Dylan's
DILEMMA

Maine Men Book Four

K.C. WELLS

Warning
This book contains material that is intended for a mature, adult audience. It contains graphic language, explicit sexual content, and adult situations.

Maine Men

Levi, Noah, Aaron, Ben, Dylan, Finn, Seb, and Shaun.
Eight friends who met in high school in Wells, Maine.
Different backgrounds, different paths, but one thing
remains solid, even eight years after they graduated –
their friendship. Holidays, weddings, funerals,
birthdays, parties – any chance they get to meet up,
they take it. It's an opportunity to share what's going
on in their lives, especially their love lives.

Back in high school, they knew four of them were gay
or bi, so maybe it was more than coincidence that they
gravitated to one another. Along the way, there were
revelations and realizations, some more of a surprise
than others. And what none of the others knew was
that Levi was in love with one of them...

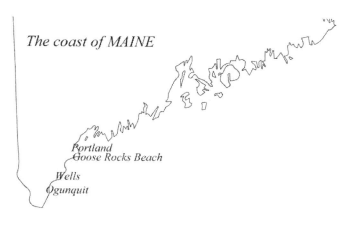

The coast of MAINE

Portland
Goose Rocks Beach
Wells
Ogunquit

Prologue

From Seb's Summer:

"But that's what's so awesome about this lot. There's always someone to turn to if you need a helping hand, or just someone to listen." Ben gazed warmly at Finn and Dylan. "I don't know what I'd have done if these guys hadn't had my back. They visited me, they took my calls, even when it was the early hours of the morning." His eyes twinkled. "Of course, Dylan said he was working the night shift at reception at the hotel at the time, but we know what he was really doing."

Finn blinked. "Speak for yourself. I don't know what he was doing."

"Watching porn on his phone," Ben said in a stage whisper.

Dylan's jaw dropped. "I never said that."

Ben guffawed. "You didn't have to. But what I want to know is... was it het porn or gay porn?"

"Ben can want all he likes," Finn said to Dylan in a firm voice. "You don't have to tell him anything. Because it's none of his business what you watch—isn't that right, Ben?" He gave Ben a hard stare.

Ben flushed. "You're right. Sorry, dude." He got up and went over to the other couch where Wade, Aaron, and Noah were still talking. Dylan's cheeks were red.

Marcus had the impression Ben had hit a nerve.

"Did you say we get a room to ourselves?" Joel asked Finn. When Finn nodded, Joel's eyes sparkled. "Want to show

me where it is?"

Finn was on his feet in a heartbeat. He grabbed Joel's hand and tugged him up off the couch, then led him toward the door.

Dylan coughed again. "Well, that was subtle." He got up and took Joel's place on the couch. "Listen, about what Ben said—"

Marcus held up his hand. "Before you say another word, can I point something out? Finn was right. What you watch is no one's business but yours."

"Yeah, but he makes it sound like I was watching porn when I should've been working. I'd get fired for that."

Marcus arched his eyebrows. "The night shift at a hotel reception desk? That has to be one of the deadest shifts going, right?"

Dylan nodded. "And it's just me. A guy could get bored to death just sitting there." He nibbled on his lower lip. "And about that other thing he said…"

Marcus had a feeling he knew what was bothering Dylan. "Doesn't matter if you watch guys with girls, girls with girls, guys with guys… whatever helps." He leaned in. "I may be gay, but I've watched straight porn."

Dylan blinked. "Really?"

Marcus nodded. "Of course, I was pretty much focused on the guys' asses and dicks."

Dylan chuckled. "Some of their cocks are huge," he whispered. "Sometimes I take one look and I swear, it hurts just thinking about taking it." His eyes widened. "Not that I have. Taken one, I mean. I'm not gay."

Marcus had been around long enough to spot a bi-curious guy with relative ease. And judging by Dylan's rapid blinking, the way he tugged on his lip, his knee that bounced as he sat beside Marcus, this was one very nervous, curious man.

"It's okay, you know," he said in a low voice. When

Dylan froze, Marcus nodded. "It's okay to be curious. And if the opportunity should arise to be more than curious? Don't panic about it. I have a nephew, in his early twenties, and recently I gave him this advice. I told him he needed to decide which was

better to live with—the regret of doing something, or not doing something."

Dylan's breathing quickened. "It's like that FOMO they all talk about. You know, fear of missing out? Well, sometimes I wonder if I'm not missing out on... something."

Marcus smiled. "Mark Twain once wrote some very wise words. Let me see if I can remember them correctly." He paused, then recited, "'Life is short, break the rules, forgive quickly, kiss slowly, love truly, laugh uncontrollably and never regret anything that made you smile.' Everyone always quotes that bit, but he goes on to say 'Twenty years from now you will be more disappointed by the things you didn't do than the ones you did. So throw off the bowlines. Sail away from the safe harbor. Catch the trade winds in your sails.'" Marcus paused. "He ended with three words. 'Explore. Dream. Discover.'"

Dylan swallowed. "Sounds like he was a very wise man."

Chapter One

Explore. Dream. Discover.

Simple enough instructions, but not so easy to put into practice.

Three little words that had been echoing in Dylan Martin's head ever since Marcus Gilbert had uttered them a mere two hours before.

Three little words preventing Dylan's brain from shutting down, no matter how much he wanted to sleep.

Three little words he yearned to embrace.

After he'd lain awake in bed for about an hour, Dylan gave up on the idea of sleep. It just wasn't happening. Shaun was out like a light, and from the other couch came the sound of Levi and Noah's mingled breathing, deep and even.

Dylan envied them. They'd all hit the sack about two o'clock, and he reckoned the others had fallen asleep within minutes.

He knew what was keeping his brain from shutting down, however.

He eased out from under the sheets, grabbed his phone from the coffee table, and padded barefoot into the kitchen. Once inside, he closed the door, then headed for the fridge. He peered at the bottles of water and cans of soda before settling on a bottle of iced tea. Marcus's words played on a loop in his head, and he found himself dissecting and analyzing them.

Love truly. Dylan was honest enough to admit he'd never done that. There had been infatuations, crushes, sure, but love? That one had eluded him so far.

Forgive quickly. Dylan wasn't one for holding a grudge—except for when it came to his family, and God knew, they'd done nothing to warrant his forgiveness.

Kiss slowly. That made him smile. *Is there any other way?*

Laugh uncontrollably. The guys never failed to make him smile, and they'd shared a lot of laughs throughout the years, but as for uncontrollably? *When was the last time I laughed till I cried?*

Never regret anything that made you smile. Most of Dylan's regrets were centered on stuff he hadn't done. *And wasn't that what Marcus was trying to say? About which regret was better to live with?*

Watching Finn, Ben, and now Seb find their own happiness should have made *him* happy, but instead what ate him up was envy, and he *hated* that. It made him feel mean-spirited and unclean.

So what if they've found someone? It doesn't mean their lives are better than mine, right? Or that they're having more fun than I am?

Deep down, that was *exactly* how it felt, and he loathed himself for even thinking that way.

He sat at the small kitchen table, the opened bottle before him, staring at the velvet blackness pressing against the window. When the low noises first reached his ears, Dylan wasn't certain what he was hearing, until he realized the kitchen window was open, and Ben and Wade were sleeping in a tent in the back yard.

Except they weren't sleeping.

Dylan told himself it was wrong. He shouldn't have been listening to Wade making love to his friend, but he couldn't stop himself. It was obvious who was doing what, but it wasn't the whispered instructions that sent a tide of heat crawling up Dylan's bare chest, reaching his neck and face.

It was the soft sounds of two men enjoying each other, lost in their own little world, and it was hotter and more intimate than anything Dylan had encountered.

Stop this.

He got up from his chair, crept over to the window, and closed it, shutting out the erotic soundtrack. He glanced at his phone on the table.

I shouldn't.

Why not? They're all asleep. They won't know.

Dylan scrolled to find his favorite site, knowing precisely what he was searching for. Except it was more of a *who*. He typed a name into the search field, his heart beating as fast as a hummingbird's wings. When he saw a new upload, his heart pounded so hard, he felt sure everyone in the house could hear it.

There was a new Mark Roman video, and Dylan had left his earbuds in the living room. *Fuck.* He switched the phone to silent and clicked on the video.

Autopilot was still engaged as he reached into his shorts and curled his hand around his stiffening cock, his gaze locked on the screen. He propped his phone on its side against the salt and pepper shakers, and shoved his shorts past his hips.

Mark was on a king bed, lying on his back,

stroking his thick shaft, and his sexy smile made something quiver in Dylan's belly.

That is one hot man.

Dylan could have described Mark with his eyes closed. He'd stared so many times at Mark's upswept hair, longer on top with a hint of highlights, but short on the side, mostly silver. Those cool blue eyes seemed to peer right into Dylan's soul. His goatee was peppered with silver too, and there was a hint of stubble along his firm jawline. Mark's abs spoke of his dedication to looking good, as did the curve of his arms and the swell of his pecs.

Don't forget that tattoo. Just seeing the words *Fuck Me* on Mark's firm ass cheek was enough to give Dylan palpitations.

The camera angle changed, and Dylan's cheeks burned as he watched Mark's screen partner give head. The camera gave the perfect view down Mark's torso to his dick, which glistened as the other guy took him deep. Dylan's cock ached as Mark pumped his hips, thrusting up into the guy's mouth.

Would it feel all that different to a girl's mouth?

It wasn't the first time the thought had occurred to him, and he doubted it would be the last. The guy was clearly relishing his task, and even with no sound, it was hot as fuck. What made it hotter was their reflection in the mirror behind him.

Then Dylan heard the quiet *snick* of a door, and he yanked up his shorts and exited the video, his heart racing. He breathed deeply, forcing calm into the turbulence.

Shaun poked his head around the door, then came into the room. "Couldn't you sleep?" he whispered. He closed it behind him.

"I thought you were dead to the world."

"Bad dream." Shaun shivered.

Dylan gestured to the bottle in front of him. "There's iced tea, soda and water if you're interested."

Shaun went over to the fridge and removed a bottle of water, then joined him at the table.

Dylan studied him. "You were very quiet tonight." It didn't take a genius to work out why.

Shaun focused on his bottle. "Yeah. Things... things aren't good right now. Christ, I was so torn about this weekend. I haven't been away from Dad since Grammy's birthday party in June, and you have *no* idea how much I needed this. But at the same time..." He swallowed. "Not that he'll realize I've been gone."

"Is it that bad?" Dylan knew very little about dementia.

"I think he's reached stage six. I wasn't sure how long it would be before we got there, but it kinda came at us like a Mack truck."

"What's stage six?"

Shaun sighed. "You don't want to hear about this."

"Maybe not, but it seems to me that you *need* to talk about it. And I talked *your* ear off enough times when we were seniors in high school, so I think I can be here for you now." Shaun and the others had been Dylan's lifeline, his refuge from the passive-aggressive prison he'd lived in.

Not that I knew back then what passive-aggressive even meant. Realization had come later.

Shaun took a long drink before speaking. "I know more about dementia than I ever wanted to. There are seven stages, and six of them all have the words *cognitive decline* in their title. The thing is, there's no rhyme or reason as to how fast a person moves between stages. So many factors have to be taken into account." Another drink. "He'd been at stage five for a long time. That was when he needed help dressing and bathing. That was also when I employed the first in-home nurse."

"Didn't you tell us about his new in-home nurse? It's a guy, right?"

Shaun nodded. "Nathan. He's great. I couldn't cope without him."

"So what's different about stage six?"

Shaun's face tightened. "Then, he was getting more and more confused or forgetful. But now… Dad's not sleeping well. He gets into these… loops of obsessive behavior, like when he wants to tell me about something that happened forty years ago when he was a teenager, but he tells the same story over and over." He swallowed. "He has these bursts of paranoia, and he won't listen when I tell him everything's fine. It feels like he's always worrying about something. And…" There was pain in Shaun's eyes, and Dylan ached to see it there. "Last week, he… he looked right at me and said 'Who are you?'" He lowered his gaze. "This is what they call Severe Cognitive Decline, and suddenly we're only one step away from Very Severe. And when *that* happens…"

Dylan couldn't speak. There was nothing he could say to ease Shaun's suffering, and he didn't want to offer trite words. His face tingled.

I'm sitting here, worrying if I'm missing out on stuff, and meanwhile, Shaun is going through hell. It put Dylan's feelings into sharp relief.

"How about we try to get some sleep?" he

suggested. "Because you *know* Aaron will be up with the birds, making breakfast and demanding we all get out of bed. And then it'll be no time at all before Seb is grilling up a storm for lunch."

Shaun's sad smile made his stomach clench. "I wasn't sure about staying for lunch, to be honest. We'll see. But you're right. We should try to get a few hours' sleep."

Dylan picked up his phone and followed him out of the kitchen, both of them creeping into the living room. He climbed beneath the sheets, and Shaun got in on the other side. On impulse, Dylan reached across and found Shaun's arm. He squeezed it.

"I know there's nothing I can say that will make your situation any better," he whispered, "but… if you ever need me—whether it's just a chat on the phone, or even a hotel room for the night when you need a break—I'm here for you. Okay?"

Shaun's hand covered his. "Thanks, man. I really do appreciate it."

Dylan lay on his back, listening to the change in Shaun's breathing as he finally fell asleep. *Poor guy.* Shaun had a hard row to hoe: once his dad had started along this path, they'd all known it was going to be a downward slope, one that would lead to an unhappy ending. And all they could do was be there for him.

His mind went back to the video he'd been watching. Something about it niggled him, and for the life of him, he couldn't work out what felt odd. In exasperation, he reached down to the floor where he'd left his phone, then tugged the sheets over his head: he didn't want its light to wake the others.

Dylan scrolled to the video again, starting from

the beginning. It was only when Mark stood to fuck his partner that he realized exactly what had messed with his head, and he gaped at the screen.

They shot this in my hotel. I know *that room.*

Chapter Two

August 30

Dylan added a heap of potato salad to his plate, then helped himself to pickles and salsa.

"You sure you got enough there?" Ben teased. He held up the bowl of potato salad. "Why not just take the lot and be done with it?"

"Leave him be." Seb paused in his task of turning the burgers and chicken fillets. "That's Grammy's recipe, isn't it?" When Levi nodded, Seb grinned. "Enough said. Get it while there's still some left." He glanced at Marcus's plate and smirked. "Smart man. You already did."

Dylan headed for the nearest empty chair. Brunch was a free-for-all, with grilled meat, salads, even mac and cheese. Buckets of ice stood around the small yard, filled with soda, water, iced tea, and of course beer, though it was a little early in the day for him. Every available seat was out there.

We've gone from eight to eleven. Dylan couldn't help wondering if more of them were going to find partners. *This seems to be the year for it.* Seb was the biggest surprise of all. Dylan didn't think he'd ever get over the shock of Seb settling down. Marcus looked as though he was a pretty good match.

"Hey, Aaron. You got anything planned for after brunch?" Finn demanded. His eyes twinkled. "As long as it's not climbing Mount Champlain, I'm in."

"I thought we could take it easy this time." Aaron glanced at the sky. "It's such a beautiful day, I thought we could all go to the beach. Sand Beach is right around the corner, and it's a great spot."

Wade nodded. "Ben and I went there this summer with my nephew. We had a wonderful time."

"So I thought we could take a ball, my Aerobie ring, whatever, and hang there for a while before everyone goes home."

"Would it be okay if *some* of us just sat on a towel and *watched* all those activities?" Marcus asked. "Not that I'm averse to a little exercise, but—"

"Lemme guess," Ben interjected. "Seb kept you… busy all night, and you have no energy left." He heaved an exaggerated sigh. "Some people have no stamina." Wade dug him in the ribs with his elbow, and Ben stared at him. "What? I'm up for a little beach action, and I probably got less sleep than most of these guys." He grinned. "As you well know."

Wade coughed and his face turned red.

"Can I borrow one of your paddle boards?" Seb asked Aaron.

"Sure. I was gonna take one anyway. I've got a spare wet suit too if you're interested. We can ride some waves."

Seb leaned over and kissed Marcus on the lips. "*You* get to watch me make a fool of myself out there."

Marcus stroked Seb's cheek. "I am *never* going to think you're a fool. In my dictionary under *perfect*, it says, 'See Seb Williams.'"

Noah let out a sigh. "That is freaking adorable."

Dylan couldn't help noticing how Levi's face tightened just a tad. *What's his problem?*

Marcus came over and sat beside Dylan. "Hey." He took a forkful of the potato salad and his eyes widened. "Oh my God."

Dylan chuckled. "I know. Grammy's a freakin' genius when it comes to cooking. Except… she's a pretty cool all-rounder."

"I must meet her one day. Seb has mentioned her a few times."

Dylan smiled. "I'm sure you'll meet her. Maybe Halloween? Grammy throws a wicked party every year."

"Guys?" Shaun got up from his chair. "It's been great, but I've gotta go."

Aaron gave him a hug. "Thanks for coming. And give my love to your dad."

"I will. I'll wait for a moment when he's thinking clearly. He still gets them, just not very often these days."

"Take care, Shaun," Dylan called out. "And remember what I said."

Shaun smiled. "I will. And thanks. I might take you up on that offer one of these days." He waved to everyone, and Aaron accompanied him into the house.

"Sounds like Shaun has a lot on his plate," Marcus murmured.

"His dad has dementia, and he's gotten worse recently. Shaun's all he's got." Dylan took a peek around them. All the others were engaged in conversations. He leaned in closer. "About our conversation last night. I want to thank you."

"What for? Talking to you?"

"What you had to say was important. And you

gave me something to think about. In fact, I was thinking about it most of the night."

Marcus's eyes were kind. "I don't think what I had to say was all that thought-provoking."

"You just made me look at my life, that's all. But those were three hard-hitting words. *Explore… dream… discover.*"

Marcus tilted his head. "Have I set you off on a voyage of exploration?"

Dylan's face grew warm. "Maybe, maybe not." The conversation with Marcus had been the most he'd ever shared. Not one of the guys knew what went on inside Dylan's head. "But maybe exploration is what I need to be thinking about," he confessed.

"Where do you live?"

"Wells. I share a house with three other guys who work in the hotel."

Marcus smiled. "I'm not that far from there. You know that little place where Seb was banished for the summer? Well, that's where I am right now, until I find a place of my own. But Cape Porpoise is only about half an hour from Wells. So… If you need to talk, come see me." Marcus pulled his wallet from his jeans pocket, opened it, and took out a card. "Ignore the office number. That's my cell underneath. You can call me, or you can come over and we can sit down over a coffee or a beer or something. I work from home now, so I'm there most of the time." His eyes sparkled. "And if it's during the semester, Seb won't be around in case it's something you'd rather he doesn't hear."

Dylan couldn't help smiling. "You know, for someone who's only just met us, you have a really good handle on the situation."

Marcus shrugged. "I saw how you were last night when we talked. I know they're your friends, but that doesn't mean they can't get under your skin. And it might be easier to talk to someone who's a relative stranger, instead of people you've known most of your life."

"You might be right about that." In fact, Marcus had nailed it. There was so much Dylan kept to himself, even though he'd been around these guys since junior high. He'd spent most of his life being a very private person. Unburdening himself to Marcus had been out of character.

Marcus gave him a warm smile. "Well, now you have my number. Use it if you feel the need. I'm a good listener."

"You're pretty good when it comes to giving advice too." And Dylan could always use another friend.

The sand was warm beneath his bare feet, and the sun was hot on his head. Finn and Joel walked along the shoreline, holding hands, and the sight made Dylan's throat tighten. Wade and Ben lay together on a beach towel, talking in low voices. Levi and Noah tossed an Aerobie back and forth, and every now and then it ended up in the surf. Aaron was out on his paddle board with Seb, the pair of them watching for the next wave. Marcus sat on the towel, leaning back on his hands, his gaze focused on Seb.

Summer's at an end. Not that Dylan had done much with his summer, except work. He couldn't remember the last time he'd taken a vacation. It *might* have been when he was still living at home.

I've gotten into a rut, haven't I?

Marcus had been right. A little exploration was called for.

Then he remembered what had niggled him that night. That video had opened a whole can of worms, and Dylan didn't want to deal with it.

"Are you okay?" Seb stood in front of him, water beading on his wet suit, his hair slicked back. Aaron stood a little farther away, toweling off his hair.

"Huh?"

Seb knelt on the sand, catching the towel Marcus threw to him. "Thanks, babe." He returned his attention to Dylan. "You seem kinda distracted."

"I have something on my mind. Kind of a problem I need to solve."

"Can we help?" Ben sat up.

"I'm not sure." Sharing his thorny issue might reveal more than Dylan was prepared to bring into the light of day.

Seb sat cross-legged on the towel next to Marcus, peeling the suit down to his waist. "Well, tell us what the problem is, and we'll put our heads together."

"What Seb said," Aaron added, sitting on his damp towel.

Tell them. He didn't need to go into details, after all.

"Okay, before we go any further, I'm gonna

assume that every one of us here at some point or other has watched porn, right?"

Seb gaped. "Oh my God. You're gonna do porn."

Dylan rolled his eyes. "For Christ's sake, can you be sensible for a minute?"

Seb straightened his features. "Okay. This is me being sensible, so make the most of it. To answer your question, yes, but I don't think that's any great surprise, coming from me, right?"

"Hey, I watch porn," Aaron admitted. "I'm not gonna deny it. Nothing wrong with that. So what's the problem?"

Dylan took a deep breath. "Okay. There's this porn star I follow. I watch all of her movies." His chest constricted a little at the lie. "Well... While I was watching her most recent one, I noticed something. The room she was filming in looked kinda familiar. And then I realized why. They were filming in my hotel."

Ben grinned. "Hey, this could be your big chance, Dylan. I can see the script now. 'Server knocks on the door, and ends up fucking the sexy guest.'" His eyes gleamed. "You could have a whole new future. Probably pays better than working in the hotel too."

Wade cleared his throat. "I don't think you're helping." He addressed Dylan. "So what's the problem?"

"The thing is, my manager... He's... He has this rule. He's been manager there for God knows how long, and the hotel's reputation means a lot to him. So, everyone who gets taken on has to swear that if they see *anything* that would damage that reputation, they have to report it." Dylan sighed. "*This* is my problem. She isn't doing any harm. She's just making a living. But if I tell him, and he catches her the next time…"

Seb scowled. "This manager… Is he the same asshole who objected to a guest hanging a pride flag from their balcony last year?"

"Yeah, that's him. His excuse was it was a safety hazard." Dylan rolled his eyes.

"Then I say tell him nothing. He'd object to *any* sex being filmed in his hotel." He shook his head. "The guy walks as if he has a flagpole up his ass. See, I can say that, because I've stayed in the hotel." He peered at Dylan. "I'm right, aren't I?"

Dylan tried to keep a straight face. "Yeah."

"I take it this porn star is cute?" Ben inquired. "You got the hots for her, or something?"

Fuck, that was close to the mark.

"I just don't want to be the one to lose her some business. And what if he discovers what's going on? I could get into trouble."

Ben frowned. "How? He can't prove you knew anything about it." He gave Dylan a sympathetic glance. "I think you're overthinking this. But I agree with Seb. Don't tell the fucker anything." He raised his water bottle. "Here's to all sex workers and porn stars… long may they get us off."

Wade burst out laughing. "You really don't have a filter, do you?"

"Besides, who's to say she'll come back to the hotel to film there again?" Aaron remarked. "That might have been a one-off."

Dylan hoped so.

Aaron heaved a heavy sigh. "I hate to be the one to bring an end to this, but you've all got a long drive ahead of you. Apart from Ben and Wade, that is." His expression grew gloomy. "Work tomorrow. More Massholes to deal with. The season can't end fast enough for me." He peered at Dylan. "Things will get quieter for you too, no doubt."

Dylan nodded. "After Labor Day, sure. Then we'll be gearing up for Halloween."

Seb patted Marcus's knee. "You should see the hotel then. Cobwebs, spiders, witches, skeletons... It looks amazing."

Dylan cackled. "Let's hope you're still saying that come Halloween, because it'll probably be me who's doing the decorating this year. Gotta earn that supervisor's pay, right?"

"I'm sure you'll do a wonderful job," Marcus said warmly. Then he glanced at Seb. "You'll never catch me saying no to a night in a hotel."

"I worked that much out last night," Seb said with a grin.

Dylan wasn't really listening—he was too busy thinking about Mark Roman. As much as he'd love to see him in the flesh, as it were, he didn't want Mark anywhere near that hotel.

Find some other place to shoot porn, okay?

Chapter Three

August 29

Mark Roman took a last look around. Casey was due at any minute.

Anyone would think I was nervous. Which was understandable, seeing as the only person who visited Mark was the mailman. It had taken him almost a year to get used to this quiet corner of Wells, but now it had become his retreat, the one place where he could be himself. He didn't miss the noise and bustle of big city life: he still got to experience that when he traveled for a shoot. And when he was done, it was back to Wells, and solitude.

Of course, there was another reason for his nervous state. He hadn't seen Casey for a long time, and he was at a loss to know why he'd agreed to him staying the weekend. Intrigue, perhaps? Only, it was more than that.

Mark wanted to see him again.

The sound of a car engine spurred him into activity, and he hurried to open the front door, remaining under the porch roof as Casey parked in front of the double garage doors. He waved as he got out of the car, then walked around to the trunk to grab his bag.

"You found it then."

Casey laughed. "You weren't kidding when

you said it was off the beaten path."

"Hey, it's not that bad." Mark waited, his heartbeat quickening as Casey strolled toward the wooden steps leading up to the front door. He held out his hand, but Casey ignored it and drew him into a hug.

"Damn, it's good to see you," Casey murmured.

Mark's throat seized. He hadn't expected Casey's arrival to have such an emotional impact. He swallowed hard. "You too." His voice cracked a little. When Casey relinquished his hold, Mark opened the door and led him inside.

Casey gazed with obvious interest at the interior. "So is it you or the previous owner who has a thing for pine?"

Mark laughed. "When I was house-hunting, I lost count of how many properties had pine-clad walls. It must be a Maine thing. Or at least, a rental house thing. I think this was once a summer place in a previous life." He took Casey's bag and placed it on the floor next to the couch. "You want the full tour or the expurgated version?"

"I'll settle for the five-cent tour. I need a coffee. I've been driving for four hours, and I didn't want to stop along the way."

"In that case, the tour can wait. I'll make some coffee." He walked into the large kitchen, Casey following.

He smiled when he saw Mark's pans hanging from a rack. "Oh my God. You learned to cook? Mr. Why-bother-to-cook-when-you-can-eat-out-every-night?" When Mark gave him the finger, Casey burst out laughing. "Yeah. That's the Mark I know."

"Yes, I learned to cook. I also make my own bread."

"You bake too?" Casey blinked. "Okay, I take it back. You're nothing like the Mark I knew."

In more ways than you could know.

"How long have you had this place?"

"Three years." He bit back the words that were right there on his tongue. *And this is the first time you've visited.* "It isn't huge, but it's plenty big enough for me." Then he realized Casey was scanning the room. "What are you looking for?"

He grinned. "Cameras."

It was Mark's turn to laugh. "You won't find any. I don't shoot here." He went to the coffee pot and filled the reservoir with water, then spooned coffee into the filter.

"Why not? You could claim it as a business expense."

Mark leaned against the countertop and folded his arms. "Well, for one thing, I go where my partners are. Gotta clock up those points, right? Which is why we ran into each other in Atlanta last year, after all. And if I'm shooting in Maine, I go to a hotel." He gestured to the kitchen. "This is home."

"Home is home, work is work, and never the twain should meet, right?" Casey pulled out a chair and sat at the oval table. Then his eyes widened. "Hey, wait a minute. You *do* shoot here. I've seen your solo videos."

Mark joined him and sat. "That's not work though—that's me doing what we *all* do, only, I do it on camera. And all they get is a close-up of my cock, my hole, or both." In his mind, it wasn't the same thing as bringing guys back to shoot video. He looked

Casey up and down. "You've put on a little weight since last year. It suits you." He seemed happy too. Mark was glad of that.

"It must be love," Casey said with a smile. He cocked his head to one side. "You don't regret leaving the studios?"

"Nope. I prefer being my own boss." Except that brought with it a pile of headaches. Then Casey's words hit home. "Wait a sec. How do *you* know I don't work for a studio anymore?" He grinned. "First the comment about my solos, then me working for myself... Are you stalking me again, Mr. Ryan?"

"What? I never—" His face reddened. "Oh come on, that was seven years ago. And I wasn't stalking you. I was just... following you."

Mark nodded. "On Facebook, Twitter, Instagram, Tumblr, my website, my blog... Have I missed anything?"

"Well, if I hadn't, we would never have met."

Mark couldn't argue with that. They'd been the happiest two years of his life.

Casey peered at the pile of envelopes on the table, and frowned.

"Something wrong?"

"Just surprised to see mail addressed to Mark Roman, that's all."

He chuckled. "Yeah, go figure. Who else would it be addressed to?" Then he leaned over and pressed a finger to Casey's lips. "Don't say that name. He doesn't live here." He withdrew it slowly.

"*He*? It was *your* name."

"But that was a whole other lifetime ago. I left him behind when I left Wyoming. Hell, they said being gay was a choice, didn't they? So... I chose to be Mark

Roman."

Casey's brow was still furrowed. "I take it that situation hasn't changed?"

"Nope. They still want nothing to do with me, and I still think fuck them." He shoved all thoughts of his family aside. They would only ruin his day. "You look good."

Casey snorted. "You look better. I saw one of your early movies the other day. Hardly recognized you."

"See? You *are* still stalking me." Mark laughed. "Let me guess. I was this skinny kid who kept glancing at the camera."

"And now look at you." Casey's eyes sparkled.

"I'm not sure an engaged man should be looking at me like that."

"I can look at you any way I please. Lee's too far away to see me looking." He gestured to Mark's chest and arms. "I can't imagine how many hours you spend in the gym."

Mark glanced at the coffee pot, then stood. "Come with me." He led Casey through the house to the connecting door to the garage.

Casey's breathing hitched as he stepped through the doorway. "Wow."

Mark had filled half the space with weights, a treadmill, an elliptical trainer, a rowing machine, and whatever other equipment had caught his interest.

Casey followed Mark down the three steps into the garage. "I don't know if you've ever heard of it, but they have this thing now. It's called a gym membership?"

Mark rolled his eyes. "And *there's* the Casey I knew." He flung out his arm to encompass the equipment. "Here I can work out with no fear of someone coming up to me when I'm sweating like a pig, and saying, 'Don't I know you? Aren't you Mark Roman? Can I take a selfie with you?'"

Casey ran his hand over the elliptical trainer. "You were getting that five years ago when we were together. Didn't seem to bother you."

Mark heaved a sigh. "That was then. Growing tired of it now." When Casey stared at him, Mark shook his head. "I'm not going to go there. We have other things to talk about." A change of topic was in order. "It's good to see you. Even better to see you so happy."

"Does it show?" Casey gazed at the white gold ring on his left hand.

"I saw your post. Have you set a date yet?" Casey regarded him with wide eyes, and Mark chuckled. "Yes, I follow you on Facebook. Not that surprising, is it? You accepted my friend request, after all."

"Sure, but that was seven years ago. I didn't think you'd still be interested in my life, not when yours is far more exciting."

"I'm not certain 'exciting' is the word I'd use."

Casey flushed. "We're getting married at the end of October. It'll be a Halloween-themed wedding."

"Whose idea was that?"

"Lee's."

"And do I get an invite?" When silence fell abruptly, he blinked. "I guess not."

Casey's flush deepened. "I'd have you there in a heartbeat, but Lee... he's... he's intimidated by you."

"Me? What have *I* done to be so intimidating?"

"I think part of it is that he can't cope with the idea we were an item, but also—"

"Let me guess. The porn thing." Mark's heart sank. "I think that's sad."

"Can we not talk about this, please?"

"Of course." The last thing he wanted was for Casey to feel uncomfortable.

"Do you know what today is?"

Mark smiled. "Saturday. Senility hasn't set in yet, you know. I'm only thirty-five."

Casey laughed. "It's the day we met, you jerk. Seven years ago." He flashed a grin. "When you were still in your twenties and the hottest porn star around."

"I was never that," Mark protested.

"Don't sell yourself short. I'm proud of what you achieved."

"But not proud enough to stay." As soon as he'd uttered the words, he regretted them. "I'm sorry. That was a cheap shot."

"But a well-aimed one." Casey's shrug didn't ease Mark's flare of guilt.

Change the subject.

"And of course I remember. That show at Hustlaball." He grinned. "I was fucking some guy on a bed, you walked past, and said 'Nice tattoo.'"

Casey gaped. "You heard that? I never knew."

"When you walked over to me after, you seemed nervous. I didn't want to embarrass you. Then you asked if I wanted a drink. The rest, as they say, is history."

"We had a good two years, didn't we?" Casey's voice grew soft.

"Why did you hook up with me?" Mark could

still recall the look of awe on Casey's face when Mark had agreed to a date.

Casey shrugged again. "I thought I could cope with the porn. You fucking other guys. But as we now know, when it came down to it, I couldn't."

"Remember what you said to me the day we broke up?"

Casey nodded. "I said if you ever left the industry, to look me up. I do understand why you couldn't walk away from all that."

"That was then. The industry is very different now."

"Guys still watch porn though."

"Sure, but other factors come into play. *Now* we have an audience who says 'Why pay for it, when I can get it for free?' Studios are closing. Puritanical attitudes are increasing. Sex workers are finding it tough to make a living,"

"Is that how you see yourself, as a sex worker?"

Mark gazed at him in surprise. "That's what I am—and it *is* work, make no mistake. You have *no* idea what I have to do on a daily basis." He waved his hand. "But I'm not going into that now."

Casey gazed at him with a critical eye. "You look… tired."

Then it does show.

He nodded. "I am. Five years ago I couldn't have walked away. Now?" He was getting beyond tired of it all.

Casey fell silent, and the hairs prickled on Mark's nape. Then Casey leaned back. "What do you want, Mark? I mean, *really* want?"

Mark didn't hesitate. "A life." Casey arched his

eyebrows, and Mark sighed heavily. "A different life, then. I'm enough of a realist to know if I stopped now, my fans would soon forget me. There'd be a new guy to follow. And then maybe I'd be able to walk into a gay bar and not have some barely legal twink walk up to me, fondle my ass, and say 'Hey, wanna be my Daddy?'"

Casey chuckled. "You're thirty-five. Isn't that a bit young to be a daddy?"

Mark laughed. "Daddy is not an age, it's a state of mind. And *this* is hot right now." He stroked the gray on his chin and on the side of his head.

"Then walk away."

He smiled. "I'd need a destination to walk *to* first." Mark cleared his throat. "You know what? Ignore me. I'm getting morose."

"No, I just think you're being honest. Which is more than *I'm* being right now."

"What do you mean?"

That flush was back. "Lee thinks I'm visiting an aunt."

"Ah. He wouldn't like the idea of you staying with me."

"Nope."

Alarm bells started ringing. "Look, if he's *that* insecure…"

Casey held up his hand. "I love him, okay?"

"You loved me once."

He smiled. "No—I *worshipped* you. Your biggest fan, remember? That *was* how I introduced myself, wasn't it?" Casey stilled. "Did you love me?"

Mark was rendered speechless for a moment. "Didn't I say it?"

"Sure, but… I was never certain if it was just

words. I think you loved the *idea* that someone was in love with you."

Which was probably the saddest thing Mark had ever heard. "I still care for you," he murmured. "When you phoned and asked if you could visit, I didn't hesitate."

"I know. And I care for you too." Casey's face glowed. "You were the first man I ever loved. But now? I want *you* to find yourself head over heels in love." Casey met his gaze. "You said you wanted a life. Maybe love is what comes after." He cast a longing glance toward the kitchen.

Mark chuckled. "I forgot. You're in dire need of coffee." He led Casey out of the garage back into the main part of the house. The coffee's aroma scented the air. Mark filled two cups and returned to the table, where Casey was seated once more. "You still take yours black?"

Casey nodded. "Is that the only reason you agreed to this weekend? Because you still care for me?"

"And because I wanted to see you. A snatched moment in a bar in Atlanta didn't make up for not seeing you for four years before that. We didn't have time to talk."

Casey gave him a hard stare. "Hey, it wasn't *my* fans who kept coming up to us and interrupting." He took a drink from his cup. "So… what are we doing this weekend? What sights are you going to show me?" When Mark guffawed, Casey gave him an inquiring glance. "Did I say something funny?"

"I've lived here three years, and I've barely seen a thing." Which was pitiful when he thought about it.

Casey tut-tutted. "You were right. You do need a life. Starting today. We'll go for a walk. Or we'll get in my car and drive. I don't care which, as long as I get you out of the house."

Mark sipped his coffee. "Are you trying to reform me?"

"I'll do anything if it makes you smile."

The sincerity in Casey's voice tightened Mark's chest.

Casey covered Mark's hand with his. "I meant to ask you the last time we met, but I didn't have the nerve—or the time. Tell me you haven't been alone since we split up. Tell me there have been other guys."

"There have been a few. They'd last a couple of weeks, maybe months, and then we'd hit the same stumbling block."

"Your career?"

He nodded. "Ironic, huh? They'd want me to give up the porn, and I didn't want to. And yet now…" His phone buzzed, and he pulled it from his pocket. When he saw Rich's name, he sighed. "I have to make a call. Sorry, but this is work."

"Go make your call. I'm not going anywhere."

Mark got up from the table and wandered into the living room. He hit *Call.* "Hey."

"Just checking. You still wanna do a foursome scene? Because I've found two guys who are interested."

"Who are they? Do I know them?"

"Maybe? Austin Reno and Mickey Tate."

Mark recognized the names instantly. He laughed. "Oh, I know them, all right. We've filmed together before." He made a mental note to pack the ropes and cuffs: Austin and Mickey would be up for a kinky shoot. "And they'd be prepared to come to Maine?"

"Sure. Same as last time?"

"Yep."

"Okay. Text me the date when you've booked a room, and I'll sort out the rest. This one might take a while. I've seen these guys in action." Rich cackled. "Can you say *ka-ching*?"

Mark chuckled. "I know—I was *in* that action. I'll get right on it. Thanks, Rich."

"Hey, I owe you. That was one smoking scene we did last time."

Mark said goodbye and disconnected. As he walked back into the kitchen, Casey smiled. "I take it you're not ready to walk away just yet."

He couldn't do that. Right then he only had one iron in the fire. He'd need a few more before he could contemplate leaving it all behind.

Maybe Casey's right. Maybe once I've started over, I'll find someone. Because he didn't want to wait till he was old and fully gray before he found a partner. *Face it, Mark. You're lonely as fuck.*

Sometimes that inner voice didn't pull any punches.

Chapter Four

September 5

Dylan had known from experience that come Labor Day weekend, the hotel would be busy, but even he had to admit, this beat all records. From the moment he stepped behind the reception desk, he'd been inundated with guests checking out, ensuring rooms had been turned over, dealing with lost keycards... Terry who worked the shift with him was looking the worse for wear, and Dylan could hazard a guess what *that* was all about. When they got a lull, he leaned in and whispered, "Dude. Take a break, and while you're on it, find some toothpaste or mouthwash. And mints. Strong coffee might be a good bet too." He'd spotted Mr. Reynolds, the manager, hovering in the lobby. If Reynolds got so much as an inkling that Terry was hung over, Terry's ass would be grass, and Reynolds would be a fucking *lawnmower.*

Terry had spotted Mr. Reynolds too, judging by the start he gave. "Aw thanks, Dylan. You're a lifesaver."

"Just remember you owe me one," Dylan whispered as Terry scooted out from behind the desk. "And don't take too long, okay?" Terry waved as he scurried across the marble floor, ducking as he passed the manager, who thankfully was speaking with a couple of guests.

Dylan shook his head as he straightened up the desk. Mr. Reynolds would have something to say about that too. He opened the drawer below to check they had enough keycards for the next onslaught.

"Good afternoon."

Dylan jerked his head up at the familiar warm, silky voice, and had to fight to keep his jaw from dropping. *Oh my fucking God.*

Mark Roman was standing in front of him, smiling.

Dylan gave a violent cough, remembering at the last minute to do it into his sleeve. Then he straightened. "Good afternoon, sir. Do you have a reservation?"

Mark nodded. "Name of Roman."

Dylan's hands shook as he brought up the details on the monitor. "Ah yes, Mr. Roman. You've reserved a Superior King, for one night." He tapped at the keyboard. "And you've paid in advance. That's room 410." He grabbed a paper wallet, and wrote the room number and checkout date on it. Then he slid a card into the machine and hit the key, trying to keep his mind on his task and not on Mark's handsome face.

"I'm expecting guests for a meeting."

Dylan jerked his head up once more. "'A meeting'?" Damn it, the words came out as a squeak. Mark bit his lip, his blue eyes twinkling, and Dylan struggled to compose himself.

"I've stayed here before, so I know guests can't access the elevator without a keycard. I'd be very grateful if you would call me when they arrive, and I'll come down for them."

"Certainly, sir." Dylan retrieved the keycard and placed it snugly in the wallet. He printed out the room reservation, indicated where he required details with an *X*, and placed it on the desk, along with a pen. "If you could just fill this out please, and sign it?"

Mark picked up the pen in his left hand, and proceeded to write. Dylan smiled. "Another left-hander."

Mark glanced up. "'Another'? You too?" He smiled back. "Well, you know what they say… If the right side of the brain controls the left side of the body, then only left-handed people are in their right minds."

Dylan chuckled. "I have a friend whose grandmother always says, 'I may be left-handed but I'm always right.'"

"Well, if we're going to swap sayings, I've always liked 'Everyone is born right-handed. Only the greatest overcome it.'" Mark's eyes glittered. "But you know what my favorite saying is?"

Dylan found himself leaning forward, unable to resist that captivating voice. "Tell me."

Mark grinned. "'Lefties Rule.'" He handed Dylan the sheet of paper and the pen. "Is that everything?"

Dylan scanned it. "Yes, sir." He handed Mark the wallet. "Your keycard. If you want to order anything from room service, be advised there might be a short delay. The hotel is fully booked this weekend."

"Then I was fortunate to find a room. Thank you…" Mark's gaze drifted lower to where Dylan's name badge was pinned to his waistcoat. "Dylan." Then he bent to pick up something, straightened, and walked away.

Dylan watched his retreat, his gaze locked on that firm-looking ass. *I know what that ass looks like naked.* Then he noticed what Mark was carrying. It was a longish bag, more like the kind of bag camping gear came in.

Except he suddenly knew it didn't contain camping gear, but probably tripods, lights, and any other paraphernalia required to…

Shoot a porno. Aw fuck.

Dylan forced himself not to think about it. Whatever Mark chose to do in the privacy of his room was none of his business.

As long as Mr. Reynolds didn't find out.

Fifteen minutes later, Terry returned, smelling a damn sight mintier than he had done previously. "Better?" Dylan asked with a chuckle.

"Yeah. Took something for my head too. It's pounding."

The word conjured up images that Dylan did *not* want in his head right then.

Terry's arrival coincided with a fresh wave of guests, and for the next half hour both of them worked nonstop. Terry's low whistle captured Dylan's attention, and he glanced up from the desk.

"Now *that's* how *I* wanna look," Terry murmured. "The guy must live in a gym."

The guy in question was tall, with broad shoulders, a wide chest, and a bald head that gleamed. His tee clung to his torso, and his jeans looked as if they'd been sprayed on. He wore sunglasses, which he removed as he approached the desk.

Dylan had a feeling he'd seen him before, only wearing a whole lot less clothing.

"Hi." The guy flashed him a smile. "Could you

call Mark Roman's room, please? Tell him Rich is here."

Dylan reached for the phone, his finger slipping off the keys. He started again, and after three rings, Mark answered. "Mr. Roman? Dylan from reception here. Your guest has arrived."

"Thanks. I'll be right down." He disconnected.

Dylan replaced the handset. "Mr. Roman is coming. The elevators are over there." He pointed.

"Thanks." The guy flashed him another smile, then headed across the lobby.

"He looks like he should be in movies," Terry muttered.

It was all Dylan could do not to blurt out that he already was. Thankfully, Mr. Reynolds was nowhere to be seen, so he figured the danger had passed. *As long as they don't make so much noise that a guest complains, I think they'll get away with it.*

For the next ten to fifteen minutes, they dealt with the incoming tide of guests. If the rest of the day was as busy, Dylan could see a cold beer in his future when his shift finished, and maybe he'd eat out too. He'd have earned it.

"Is there some body builders' convention at the hotel that we don't know about?" Terry whispered.

Dylan frowned. "What? I don't think so. Why do you—" He glanced up, and the words died in his throat. Two men were approaching the desk, both with bags slung over shoulders that looked as if they'd been sculpted. Both men wore tank tops and jeans, and one of them had a heavy chain around his neck, a padlock front and center resting between his collarbones. They drew glances from guests as they approached, not that Dylan was surprised by that.

Then he realized Mr. Reynolds was also watching them, his expression almost glacial.

Shit shit shit.

"I'll get this one," Dylan said quickly. He gave them a smile as they reached the desk. "Good afternoon, gentlemen."

The taller of the two cleared his throat. "Hey. We're here to meet Mark Roman. Could you call his room, please? He's expecting us."

"Certainly." Dylan grabbed the phone and dialed 410. As the call was picked up, he caught a voice in the background.

"Is this camera angle okay?"

As if he hadn't known all along.

"Hello?" That was Mark.

"Sir, two more guests have arrived."

"I'll be right down."

Dylan coughed. "Er, Mr. Roman? Will there be any more guests arriving?" *What the fuck are they shooting up there, a gangbang?* What mortified him was the fact that he even knew what a gangbang was.

Mark chuckled. "No, that's all of them. Thank you, Dylan." He disconnected.

Dylan replaced the handset. "Mr. Roman will meet you at the elevators, over there."

The guy smiled. "Thanks." They turned and ambled across the lobby, and Dylan's throat tightened when the tall one reached down and gave the other guy's ass a squeeze.

Aw fuck, please don't let Reynolds have seen that.

Mr. Reynolds stood by the fake plants, his eyes bulging.

Dylan shoved down hard on his rising panic and dealt with the next guest, his heartbeat quickening when he realized Mr. Reynolds was walking toward the desk.

Please don't ask me. Please don't ask me.

Mr. Reynolds waited until the guest had taken his keycard before beckoning Dylan with a crooked finger. "A word, if I may, Mr. Martin."

Trying his damnedest to hide his reluctance, Dylan went over to him, head held high, as if he had nothing to hide.

Mr. Reynolds stood next to the printer, out of earshot of any of the guests. "Those two... gentlemen who were here just now..." he said in a voice so low it was almost a whisper. "Are they staying in the hotel?"

Dylan struggled to maintain his composure. "They're here for a... business meeting, sir. That's what they said." He was careful to speak quietly.

Mr. Reynolds arched his eyebrows. "In that attire? I hardly think so." He narrowed his gaze. "Mr. Martin, do you have any reason to suspect that is *not* the purpose of their presence here?"

Crap. Dylan took a deep breath. "They... they might be filming a... video, sir. It's a possibility, at least."

Mr. Reynolds froze. "What kind of video?"

Dylan computed all the variables. If he didn't tell Reynolds what he suspected—which was what *anyone* would suspect just by looking at the guys—then he was in trouble. If he told... *But it's not illegal, is it? They're not harming anyone.*

Except he knew what he had to do.

"They *might* be shooting a... a... a pornographic film, sir." He wouldn't have dared use the word porno with so formal a personage as Mr. Reynolds.

The manager's eyes flashed. "And when were you going to pass on your suspicions?"

"When I'd finished dealing with the guests, sir. You can see how busy we are."

His response appeared to placate Mr. Reynolds. "Yes, I can see that. Which room are they holding their… 'meeting' in?"

"410, sir."

Mr. Reynolds turned on his heel and strode in the direction of the elevators.

Shit. Shit. If Mark was really lucky, Mr. Reynolds wouldn't call the cops.

Then he heaved a sigh of relief as a group of guests thronged around Reynolds, all talking at once. With any luck, once he'd dealt with them, this whole business might have slipped his mind.

Yeah right.

Mark laughed at the speed with which Rich, Austin and Mickey got out of their clothes and into the walk-in shower. He was already in his robe. "Don't take too long in there. I want to shoot this one while we have daylight," he quipped. He knew from experience that it could take up to four-and-a-half hours of footage to produce a forty-minute video, plus, he'd worked with Rich before.

Rich liked to take his time.

Mickey strolled out of the bathroom first, naked, his cock pointing the way. He gave it a tug. "I was thinking about getting into your fine ass all the way here."

Mark grinned. "It's all yours." When Mickey's stomach grumbled, Mark cackled. "I can see I might have to edit out all the additional sound effects. Haven't you eaten today?"

"Just something light for breakfast. I'll eat when we're done. Food only makes me sluggish." His eyes sparkled. "I've been eating pineapple for four days now."

Mark laughed. "You know that's a myth, right?"

"Really?"

"Okay, it might make a *slight* difference, being so acidic, but..." Mark shrugged. "Some foods do make it taste different. There was one guy I filmed with. His cum tasted awful. Only vegan I ever blew. Gotta make you wonder, right? Maybe meat is best."

Mickey grinned and smacked his dick on his palm. "I got some meat for ya right here."

Mark rolled his eyes.

Austin and Rich came back into the room, and Mark chuckled. "First to arrive, Rich, and last out of the goddamn bathroom." He pointed to the bed. "Start warming up, guys."

Rich got onto the mattress on all fours and spread his knees wide, ass tilted. "Are we going to plan this, or just go with the flow?"

"Option two, I think," Mark said as he checked the three tablets attached to the tripods around the bed. They only needed one ring light.

Austin stroked Rich's round bubble butt. "Is a

DP likely?"

Mark arched his eyebrows and snorted. "You've seen my stuff. What do you think?"

Austin rubbed his thumb over Rich's pucker. "I *think* this hole would look amazing with two dicks."

Rich twisted to stare at him. "Just make sure you do plenty of prep then."

"Thanks for your results, guys." They'd texted Mark with their latest tests, and confirmed they were all on PrEP. Then he laughed as Austin wasted no time, spreading Rich's ass cheeks and diving in with his tongue.

A long groan tumbled from Rich's lips. "Jesus, you're good at that."

The knock at the door made Mark jump. The men on the bed turned to stare at him, and Mark brought a finger to his lips. He went to the door and peered through the eye hole. It appeared to be the manager, or someone equally official. He signaled once more for silence, then unlocked and opened it.

The guy in the suit looked him up and down, saying nothing for a moment. Then he gazed over Mark's shoulder, and froze, his nostrils flaring. Mark followed the direction of his glance and saw—

Aw fuck. The mirror was angled in exactly the wrong direction, revealing the three men on the bed, and the three tripods placed around it, not to mention the stand with the ring light.

He turned back to the Suit, but before he could get a word out, the guy held up one hand. "Look." He kept his voice low, glancing up and down the hallway. "Legally, you can do whatever you want in a room. It's not as if anyone can stop you if you're not disturbing other guests, and you don't *appear* to be creating a safety hazard." He drew himself up to his full height of what Mark estimated was five-feet-six. "However, I've been a manager here for fourteen years, and I take the reputation of the hotel very seriously. I cannot allow something like this on my watch. I don't want to get the police involved…" His eyes flashed. "But I will if I have to."

"But if we're not breaking any laws…" Mark protested, except he knew their goose was already cremated, let alone cooked.

The manager pursed his lips. "True, but if the police do come, they will ask what you're doing, and *you* will have to explain it to them. How will that affect your… business? Can you withstand the scrutiny?"

Mark could imagine the scenario. The word would spread, and suddenly every hotel in Maine would know his face. He knew when he was beaten. He sighed. "We'll be out of here in five minutes. Will that do?"

The manager's thin smile made Mark want to smack his face, but he was only doing his job. "I knew you'd see reason. Please don't let me find you on these premises again—at least, not in similar circumstances. And now I'll leave you… gentlemen to vacate the room." He walked toward the elevators, and there was a definite swagger in his step.

Mark closed the door. "Get your clothes on, guys. This is a bust."

"Want me to find us another hotel?" Rich asked.

Mark shook his head. "Not this weekend. I was lucky to get this one. I'll take you to dinner, my treat." There was no way he would take them to the house. There were some rules he wasn't prepared to break.

Damn it.

Chapter Five

"Are you sure about dinner?" Mark had dumped his gear in the trunk, and the four of them were in the parking lot next to Rich's battered truck. "Because it feels like an awful long drive just to turn around and go back." He must have apologized at least five times since that prig of a manager had strutted toward the desk.

"If I leave now, I can meet up with Jesse. The day won't be a total bust." Rich smiled. "Besides, I'm overdue for uploading a scene. Gotta keep those dollars trickling in, right?"

"And me and Mickey are dancing at Maine Street," Austin added.

"I haven't been in there much since I moved here," Mark admitted. His first visit, he'd walked through the door, someone had hollered 'Oh my fucking God', and he'd been surrounded in a heartbeat. Mark had done plenty of gigs where there'd been crowds of guys watching him do a live show, but finding so many fans on his doorstep had been a shock.

What did I expect in a gay bar in Ogunquit? Guys knitting?

"Yeah, I can believe that. I don't cause too much of a stir." Austin's eyes sparkled. "But then again, I'm not Mark Roman." He shook Mark's hand.

"Sorry about the shoot. But you must have more lined up, right?"

"Sure." Mark had a list of guys wanting to shoot with him.

"Sorry we didn't get to fuck again." Mickey proffered his hand too. "Another time?"

"Sure." They shook. "I am *so* sorry about this."

"Will you quit apologizing? It happens. And judging by the expression on that manager's face, it probably happens more than we think." Mickey grimaced. "Did you see the look he gave us when we walked out? I guess that's one hotel you can cross off your list."

"That's one thing coastal Maine isn't short of—hotels."

Rich gave him a hug. "You okay?"

"Yeah, apart from the obvious. Why do you ask?"

"Just a feeling."

Mark sighed heavily. "I'm fine. Now get your ass out of here and go shoot some porn."

"See ya, guys." Rich climbed into his car and with a final wave, he drove out of the parking lot.

"We'd better get going too. We're not due to dance until nine tonight, but after this I could do with a drink. Of course, we *thought* we'd be staying in a nice hotel." Austin grinned.

Mark looked at them aghast. "Have you got someplace to stay tonight?" Giving them a bed for the night was the least he could do.

Austin's eyes twinkled. "Do you really think I'm not gonna end up in someone's bed?"

"It had better be a big bed, because I'll be there too." Mickey tugged on Austin's tank top.

"Come on. You're gonna buy me a beer. And dinner."

Mark didn't think there were many guys who would turn down a night of three-ways with Austin and Mickey. "Hope it's a fun night. Make sure they tuck plenty of money into your thong."

Austin snorted. "I'll be wearing a jock. More elastic to slip a bill under. Take care, Mark." They got into the car and Mickey waved as they pulled away.

Mark gave the hotel one last glance. He really liked the place, so it was a pity he wouldn't be using it again. The prospect of an evening on the couch in front of the TV didn't thrill him. *For fuck sake it's a holiday weekend.* There had to be better ways to spend it. Then he remembered a leaflet pushed through his door, from the local market. Apparently they'd been taken over and given a new lease of life, and were now serving food. Photos of home-made bread and pizza had caught his attention. It was either that, or go home and cook for himself—again.

Fuck it.

He drove home, took his gear into the house, and flopped onto the couch. It was a little early for dinner, so he switched on the TV. When he opened his eyes, he was shocked to see two hours had passed. He'd been dead to the world. Mark headed for his bedroom to change his clothes, and then grabbed his keys.

The market was within walking distance, so that meant a couple of beers. He strolled down Acorn Drive, and turn left onto Horace Mills Road. The market stood alone at the end of a quiet street, a few cars and trucks parked in front of it, with the steep-sloped roof like so many properties in the area.

Mark went through the front door and sniffed.

Something smelled good. There weren't that many tables, so he grabbed the nearest empty one and sat. One look at the menu card convinced him. Spinach pesto pizza sounded right up his alley, and they served home-made bread with their salad. He ordered his food, along with a beer, then leaned back to take in his surroundings. He wasn't surprised to find the place quiet: most people would be out celebrating.

"Good evening." A cheerful woman in a red and white check apron set a water glass in front of him, along with a bottle of beer. "Your pizza will be about fifteen minutes. We've had a rush order."

Mark gave her a warm smile. "No problem." She left the table, and Mark resumed his appraisal. In the far corner, a young man sat with his back to the wall. He was casually dressed in jeans and a tee that didn't disguise a lean figure with long legs. But it was his face that drew Mark's attention. The guy's hair was dark brown, short and neat, and his jawline was covered in scruff, with the faintest hint of a mustache.

A very sexy face, one that Mark was sure he'd seen before. Then he remembered where, and he smiled.

Well well well.

It had taken Dylan all of a nanosecond to spot Mark as he entered the market, and his heart started doing the fandango. He lowered his gaze and pretended to read the menu, not daring to look in Mark's direction for fear he'd be caught in the act of staring—or worse, drooling.

"Excuse me."

Shit. Shit. Dylan raised his chin to meet cool blue eyes. Mark stood beside his table, a beer bottle in his hand. Dylan cleared his throat. "Can I help you?"

Mark smiled. "It's Dylan, isn't it? From the hotel?" He grinned. "I have a good memory for faces."

"Hey. Yes, I remember you." The glib phrase belied his pounding heart. "What are you doing here?"

"I live not too far from here. Thought I'd check it out."

No fucking way. "You live in Wells?"

The skin crinkled around Mark's eyes. "Didn't I just say that? Are you here alone, or are you expecting anyone to join you?"

"On my own." *And please go away.* Dylan was still suffering guilt pangs.

"Would it be presumptive of me to ask if I could join you?"

You have got *to be kidding.*

"This wasn't how I intended to be spending my evening," Mark continued, and Dylan's face grew hot. Mark's eyes glittered. "But I suspect you already know about that." Dylan coughed and Mark patted him on the back. "You okay there?"

"I'm fine," he croaked.

"And after the day I've had, you wouldn't want my evening to be completely ruined, would you?"

Talk about heaping coals on an already burning fire.

Dylan gestured to the empty chair facing him. "Take a seat. Have you ordered yet?" Breathing had never been such a chore.

"Yeah. The pizza was too big a lure. What have you ordered?"

"Meatballs." Short choppy sentences didn't require much brainpower, and being this close to Mark was distracting as fuck.

Mark smiled. "I like a man who likes his meat."

He blinked. "Excuse me?" It sounded like some kind of flirty innuendo.

"Sorry. Just a remnant from a conversation today." Mark took a drink from his beer and leaned back in his chair. "So... Your manager..."

Dylan had known it was coming. "Mr. Reynolds."

Mark nodded. "I got quite a shock when he knocked on my door. You *do* know all about this, don't you?"

"Yeah. Most of the staff are talking about it." Word had gotten around fast. Someone from housekeeping had let slip that she'd seen similar *goings-on* as she put it, except she was careful not to say that in earshot of Reynolds.

"I'd love to know what gave us away. Or is he really that vigilant?"

Dylan debated lying, but his heart wasn't in it. "I... I told him what you were doing." He steeled himself for the backlash.

"You did?" Dylan nodded. "And how did *you* know?" When Dylan mumbled a response, Mark leaned closer. "I'm sorry, I didn't catch that."

"I recognized you, okay?" he blurted out. "The

minute you turned up at reception."

"Recognized me? And you ratted me out?"

"I had to!" The words came out as a wail, and a couple of the store's customers jerked their heads to stare at him. "He got suspicious when your last two *guests* turned up." Dylan hooked his fingers in the air. "So when he asked me if I knew what was going on, I… I had to tell him. If I hadn't…"

"Would he have reprimanded you?"

Dylan snorted. "And the rest. The hotel's not in a chain, you know. I've got a cousin who works in a chain hotel in Milwaukee. He says the bigger the chain, the more likely the staff is to turn a blind eye to… stuff like that. Well, Mr. Reynolds doesn't turn a blind eye to anything."

"It's okay." Mark's voice was unexpectedly gentle. "It's just one hotel. Pity though. I liked it. So…" His eyes sparkled. "Let's get back to you recognizing me."

"Do we have to?" The words slipped out before Dylan could stop them.

Mark folded his arms. "Well, it seems to me that you owe me. Of course, I do have an idea how you could make it up to me."

"How?" Dylan's heart quaked.

"I could always film you and me. *You* know…"

When Mark's suggestion registered, cold washed over him. "I'm not gay." The declaration came out way louder than he'd anticipated. He dropped his voice to a whisper. "I'm not gay."

Mark arched his eyebrows. "But you just *happen* to recognize a gay porn star?"

Aw fuck. "Okay, so I *might* have watched a few videos. That doesn't make me gay though."

"How many is a few? Two? Three?"

Dylan coughed again. "Maybe more than a few then."

"I see."

No, you don't. Please tell me you don't.

This was turning into a nightmare.

"I couldn't," Dylan whispered.

The obvious panic in his eyes had Mark backpedaling in a heartbeat. He'd met enough curious guys to know this one wasn't up for dipping his toes in the water. "That's okay," he said in a soothing voice. "How about we change the subject?"

"Sounds good to me." Dylan picked up his water glass and drank half its contents in several gulps.

"How long have you been at the hotel?" It was a safe enough question.

"Since I was eighteen. And before you ask, I'm twenty-six, almost twenty-seven."

"Then you probably know this area way better than I do."

Dylan smiled. "I grew up in Wells."

Mark was happy to see Dylan's tension finally ebbing away. "I've lived here a few years, and I've seen next to nothing. Then again, I'm not here all that much." He bit his lip. "My… work takes me all over."

As you probably know all too well.

"What brought you to Maine? You're not from around here."

"Is it that obvious?" Mark smiled. "You're right. I was brought up in Wyoming. I didn't stay there though."

"But why here? Why Wells? You could live anywhere."

"When I was a little boy, my grandparents retired here. Mind you, with their money, they could've had a place in the Hamptons, but hey, they chose Wells. I used to spend at least three weeks of every summer vacation with them. They had a house in Wells. So many summers... I guess I was happy here."

"You said they *had* a house. Don't they live here anymore?"

Mark shook his head. "No, they moved again. To Florida. I think they wanted someplace warmer." His chest tightened. "We lost my grandmother about seven years ago."

"I'm sorry. Were you close?"

"Up until then, we exchanged cards and gifts at Christmas and birthdays, which I have to say surprised me."

"Why?"

Mark didn't want to air his family's dirty linen. He didn't know Dylan well enough for that. "Grandmomma was a strong-willed individual, and she wore the pants in their home. Anyhow, there was a family... disagreement, and I was *persona non grata.* Except once she'd passed, I learned the truth. The cards and gifts were from my grandpa—he just signed them from both of them. Well, when she died, Grandpa wanted to show me that not *everyone* in my family felt the same about me."

"I'm glad."

Mark nodded. "We wrote to each other, but he was always careful not to let anyone in the family know about it. I call him every couple of months, or he calls me. In fact, we're overdue. I must get onto that." He smiled. "He's obviously having way too much fun with the other seniors in that club he belongs to."

"So you're not exactly a stranger to these parts," Dylan concluded.

"When you put it like that, I guess not. The funny thing is, I haven't thought about this place in years."

Dylan frowned. "Surely you must have memories?"

Mark took another mouthful of beer. "I know we spent a lot of time at the house, playing in the backyard." He smiled. "Next door there was a little boy. We used to talk over the fence. I'll be damned if I can remember his name though." He stroked his beard. "I know they took us to places. I seem to recall eating ice cream near a lighthouse."

Dylan grinned. "Yeah, a lot of us did that growing up. Anything else?"

"There was this beach… All I can remember is a stretch of soft sand and a line of white houses all the way along it."

"That sounds like Drake's Island Beach. Did you ever go to Wells Beach?"

Mark shrugged. "I don't remember the names. There was one beach with a whole lot of rocks. I remember scrabbling up them when the tide came in. And… one time there was a concert in a park somewhere. I remember the bandstand had this red roof that glowed in the evening sun."

Dylan beamed. "I know exactly where you were. Wells Harbor Park."

"I *think* we came here for Christmas one year. I seem to recollect walking through snow, which was piled up high against a fence, and on the other side of it was the ocean, the waves crashing over the rocks." Mark sagged into his chair. "Wow. I haven't thought about all this for so long." All those memories, locked away for safekeeping.

"Sounds like you enjoyed being here," Dylan observed.

"Maybe that's what drew me here. The one place where I was happy."

Dylan cocked his head to one side. "You know what you should do? Spend time revisiting places from your childhood. Remind yourself why you chose to live here. Who knows? Maybe when you were looking for a place to live, your subconscious gave you a prod. So yeah, go back to those places." He huffed. "And maybe I should take my own medicine."

"What do you mean?"

Dylan sighed. "I know every one of the places you mentioned, and I couldn't tell you the last time I saw any of them. I'm either working or at home."

"And where is home?"

"I share a house here in Wells with three other co-workers. It's not as if I could afford a place of my own."

"Where's your family?"

It was as if Dylan suddenly pulled down the blinds. "Here, in Wells."

Mark was no fool. He took a backward step

from the minefield he'd almost entered. "I have an idea."

Dylan's lips twitched. "I said no already, didn't I?"

He laughed. "Relax. I got the memo. You're straight." *At least, that's what you keep telling yourself.* Not that it was any of Mark's business. "But you might like this one. I don't know anyone here—except now I know you, of course. If I do as you suggest, would you be my guide?"

"Me?" Dylan gaped at him.

"Why not? You'd be a great tour guide. I bet you're always telling guests the best places to visit, right?"

"Yeah, but—"

"You said it yourself. You need to take your own medicine. And it doesn't sound as if it would taste all *that* bad. Show me what I've been missing. Even if it means going off the beaten track. There's so much of Maine I have to see." And doing it in the company of a sexy guy would be no hardship.

A sexy straight *guy, remember?* Mark wasn't about to forget Dylan's moment of panic.

Dylan chuckled. "I do have a job, you know."

"Do you get days off, or are you a full-time slave?"

That brought a laugh. "Of course I get days off. And things will be getting quieter once this weekend is over."

"That almost sounds like a yes."

Dylan regarded him in silence for a moment. Finally, he nodded. "Okay. I'll do it."

At that moment, their food arrived.

Mark raised his glass. "Here's to the beginning

of a beautiful friendship." Then the smell of freshly baked pizza filled his nostrils, and he moaned. "God, that smells good."

Talking could wait.

Dylan grinned. "I'll drink to that."

"The smell, or the friendship?" Mark's eyes twinkled.

"Both?" Then they dug in.

Dylan couldn't believe the way the conversation had turned. He'd expected recriminations and hostility, and had been met with only warmth and an offer of friendship. Dylan could always use more friends. Of course, the difference between Mark and the guys he grew up with was he didn't want to know what *they* were like in bed.

It's not as if I ever will know. He thinks I'm straight.

Except Dylan wasn't so sure of that anymore.

Chapter Six

Mark had to admit the pizza was superb. The beer had given him a buzz too, and maybe that was what prompted him to extend an invitation. Dylan hadn't asked countless questions: if anything, he'd been quiet throughout the meal, not that Mark was complaining. After learning Dylan knew who he was, Mark had expected an interrogation of sorts, and when it didn't materialize, it had come as a pleasant surprise. So pleasant, he wasn't ready for the evening to end.

He wiped his lips with his napkin. "I don't suppose you'd consider coming back to my place for a coffee?" When Dylan blinked, Mark suddenly realized how his suggestion had sounded. "Christ, that sounds like a really cheesy pickup line. Just a coffee, honest." Dylan bit his lip, and Mark played his ace. "I think accepting my invitation is the least you can do. After all, you did ruin my plans, right?"

Dylan narrowed his gaze. "Are you going to bring that up every time we meet?"

Mark grinned. "If it has the desired effect, yes." That earned him an eye-roll. "Seriously though, I'd like the company. Unless you have plans…"

Dylan studied him in silence for a moment, then gave a shrug. "No plans. And I'd never turn down coffee."

"Great. And then you can tell me your guest

horror stories." Dylan gave him an inquiring glance. "Oh, come on. You work in a hotel. I'm sure you have lots of stories to tell."

Dylan smiled. "Oh yeah."

"See?" Mark beamed.

"Okay, I'll come, but on one condition. You let me pay for your dinner."

"Why would you do that?" Then it hit him. "Hey, did I make you feel guilty?"

"No, you didn't. I was already feeling that way before you walked through the door. In fact, I've been suffering from the guilts ever since I told Mr. Reynolds what you were doing."

Mark sighed. "Look, this was not the first time I was asked to vacate a room, okay? And as episodes go, this was way less embarrassing than others I've experienced."

"Then I'll tell you my stories if you tell me yours."

Mark smiled. "Deal. And I'll pay for my own pizza." He signaled to the lady in the checkered apron for the check. It wasn't until they'd both paid and were heading out of the door that he realized just how much he didn't want to be alone.

No one should be alone on a holiday. That was just… sad.

"And now I don't regret accepting your invitation," Dylan murmured.

"Hmm?" It was only then that Mark realized he'd spoken out loud. "Oh. That wasn't for public consumption."

"It's okay, really. And I agree with you. I spend way too many holidays working, and it's sad how alone that can feel." He lapsed into silence for a moment, and Mark didn't feel the need to fill it with conversation. Horace Mills Road stretched before them, and the only sound was their boot heels on the sidewalk.

"Do you live far?" Dylan asked as they strolled.

"Not really."

"You said your grandparents had a house here. Have you been back to see it since you moved to Wells?"

"No. It wouldn't be the same. And it's not as if I remember the address. The last time I came here, I'd have been sixteen." Jesus, almost two decades ago. "I can recall how it looked, but that's about it. Have you never lived anywhere but here?"

"Nope. When I was in high school, so many kids talked about leaving Maine when they graduated. They couldn't wait to get out of here."

"But not you." Mark glanced at Dylan as they strolled.

He smiled. "No, not me, nor any of my friends. Some of us stayed in Wells, others moved farther north, but none of us have ever strayed far from the coast."

"There's something about the ocean, isn't there?" Maybe that was why Mark had loved the visits to his grandparents.

"You should see it first thing in the morning, when the sun comes up over the water, and the air is still."

"That sounds great." They turned onto Acorn Drive, and Mark pointed. "That's my place there."

"It's quieter than where I live. Having said that, no place is quiet that has four guys living in it.

There's always noise."

Mark led the way up to the front door, and fumbled in his pocket for the key. "I don't mind quiet. But sometimes…"

"I've never lived alone. Do you find you end up talking to yourself?" Dylan asked as he stepped into the house.

"Yeah, sometimes. Either that, or I put on some music." Mark indicated the couch. "Make yourself comfortable, while I start on the coffee." He walked into the kitchen.

"You know, there's an awesome walk from Ogunquit to Perkins Cove. It's even got a name—the Marginal Way—and it goes along the coast," Dylan called out. "That's the one I was telling you about."

"Is it a long walk?" Mark filled the pot with water.

"Maybe forty minutes to an hour, depending on how fast you wanna go. It passes some pretty expensive real estate and one very swanky hotel. Lots of people use it for a run or a brisk walk."

"I don't think I've visited Perkins Cove." The name didn't ring a bell.

Judging by the gasp that filtered through from the living room, Mark had just committed a sin. Then Dylan chuckled. "It *is* a bit of a tourist trap. Do you like lobster?"

"Love it."

"Well, then I have to take you there. Footbridge Lobster is *the* place to go. Forget your lobster bisque—that's strictly for amateurs."

Mark leaned against the door frame. "Why do you say that?"

"Because you only get itty bitty baby pieces of

lobster in it. Lobster stew is the real deal. It's a butter and cream-based soup, with huge chunks of lobster." Dylan cocked his head. "You ever eaten swordfish?"

"No."

"Man, they have a swordfish sandwich to die for. They coat the swordfish in seven different spices. And if you really want to tickle your taste buds, there's the famous grilled cheese."

Mark arched his eyebrows. "What's so fabulous about a grilled cheese sandwich?"

"They make their own bread, and they stuff the sandwich with chunks of lobster."

Mark held up his hands. "Okay, I'm sold. Put that on the list."

"What list?"

He grinned. "The list of places you're going to show me."

Dylan laughed. "I can do that."

"And that walk you just mentioned… when can we do that?"

"You *are* eager, aren't you?" Dylan's eyes were bright. "Okay, my next day off is Tuesday. Will you be around then?" Mark nodded, and Dylan beamed. "Great. Then let's meet up at Obed's parking lot in Ogunquit." When Mark gave him an inquiring glance, Dylan waved his hand. "Google it. The walk starts not far from there. We can arrange a time the night before."

"Then remind me to give you my number." The coffee's aroma had already begun to emerge from the kitchen.

Dylan glanced at his surroundings. "This is kinda homey. I like it."

"Me too. I haven't done a thing with it since I

bought it. Which includes getting rid of the pool table that came with it." That was in what was going to be his dining room, when Mark finally got around to it. He usually ate in front of the TV, a tray on his lap.

"Really?" Dylan's eyes lit up.

Mark figured he'd said the right thing. "Wanna play sometime?"

"Yeah."

The coffee pot beeped. "I'll be right back." Mark returned to the kitchen. "How do you like it?"

"Creamer and two sugars, please."

Mark poured the coffee and grabbed the creamer from the fridge. "So… let's hear a hotel story. Anything exciting ever happen?"

Dylan laughed. "Apart from the two prostitution busts?"

"Seriously?" He carried two cups into the living room, and set them on the coffee table.

"Mr. Reynolds was *not* a happy bunny. He wasn't the one who called the cops—that was a guest. And then there was the time I got interviewed by the FBI."

Mark gaped. "You're kidding. Why?"

"Oh, one of the guests turned out to be some guy on the run. There wasn't a lot I could tell them, to be honest." Dylan leaned against the seat cushions. "Spring Break, we always get a load of students. One year, one guy got drunk—yeah, what a surprise—and decided to jump from his window into the pool, fully clothed."

"Jesus. How high was the window? Was he okay?"

"It was the second floor, and amazingly, yes."

"Do you just work on reception?"

Dylan shook his head. "When I started, I worked as a bell-hop—I still do, when it gets real busy—and I did room service." He flushed. "That was... interesting."

"Oh really?" Mark was enjoying himself. It made a change to talk to a guy who didn't want to take a selfie, tell Mark which was his favorite Mark Roman scene of all time, or simply ask a ton of questions about porn.

When did I last have a conversation that felt so... natural?

"You wouldn't believe how many guests answer the door for room service, naked. It's like they don't even realize it. My first time doing that shift solo, there was this one guy... I'm standing there, waiting for him to sign the receipt, and all the while his boner is... inflating."

Mark chuckled. "Take it as a compliment." When Dylan blinked, he shrugged. "You're a good-looking guy." Except that was an understatement. Mark had a thing for guys with that sexy five o'clock shadow, and the line of Dylan's jaw, his eyes, his build...

Baby, you are just freaking perfect *for me.* Then he remembered. *Nope. Don't go there. You don't wanna scare the straight boy, all right?* The only straight guys Mark tangled with were the occasional gay-for-pay dudes he filmed with.

Dylan's flush deepened, and Mark regarded him with interest. "Ever had a guest hit on you?" Dylan coughed, and Mark grinned. "Gonna take that as a yes."

"There *was* this one woman... She was maybe in her late forties or fifties, really attractive... Anyway, she came to the desk one night when I was working the late shift, and asked if I'd like to… come to her room when I finished work."

"Wow. Not subtle. I take it you declined the offer."

Dylan rolled his eyes. "Duh. She was persistent, have to give her that. I got a call at one in the morning, to say her cable wasn't working, and could I come check it. The thing is? We have satellite, and it was working just fine. Then there was the time she asked for a three-a.m. wake-up call—except she wanted me to check *personally* that she was awake."

"I see what you mean about persistent." He sipped his coffee. "How did you come to be working at the hotel?"

"I'd graduated high school, and I was looking for a job, any job—I was ready to leave home. Anyway, one of my classmates, Della, said she'd gotten a job working in housekeeping at this hotel, and they were always looking for staff. She said she'd put in a good word for me with the manager. He must have liked what he heard. I've done most things—they like you to experience all aspects of the hotel—and then they made me a supervisor on reception." He gave a shy smile. "And what about you? How did you get into your… career?"

"I didn't wake up one morning and decide my lifelong dream was to be an adult performer." Mark had never meant it to be a long-term thing—that was just the way it had worked out. "In fact, I was the same as you—I left home at eighteen. I packed a suitcase with as much clothing as I could squeeze into it, took all the money I'd saved, and I bought myself a bus ticket out of there."

"Where did you go?"

Mark grinned. "Vegas."

"Why there?"

"I knew there was a porn studio in Las Vegas that produced a lot of videos featuring guys my age. I thought I could make some money while I looked for a more... realistic job." And it had also been a middle finger to his family.

"You started when you were eighteen?"

Mark studied Dylan for a moment. *Fuck it.* "Sometimes I read these real uplifting stories about LGBTQ+ kids who come out to their family, and all they get is love and support." He scowled. "That is *not* my story. When I told my parents I was gay, you know what they said to me? 'No one is born gay. It's a choice. So choose to be straight.'"

"Oh. I'm sorry. I've come across those stories too, in my own life." When Mark gave him a speculative glance, Dylan sighed. "You know I mentioned my friends? Well, there are eight of us who met in high school, some earlier than that, and we stayed friends. Four of them are gay, and of those, three came out when they were teenagers. One has a similar story to yours—that's Seb—but Levi's grandmother has been awesome. She's been a surrogate mom to a few of us, including me." He took a drink. "So... you left home, went to Vegas...."

"I went straight from the bus depot to the studio."

Dylan laughed. "You were keen."

"Thankfully, they agreed to let me audition. The usual kind of thing—jerking off for the camera, lots of photos of me flexing." He snorted. "Not that I had much to flex in those days." The body work had come later. "When some of their subscribers expressed an interest in seeing more of me, I did my first shoot, bottoming for some guy with a humongous dick. Talk about being dropped in at the deep end."

"But you stuck with it."

Mark nodded. "There aren't many guys who've stayed active in the industry for this long—I'll be thirty-six next birthday—but porn has undergone a few changes throughout those years. I went from studio to studio, learning as much as I could."

"This is fascinating. What did you learn?"

Mark chuckled. "How to fuck a guy from the right angle so that the camera captures my cock. How not to get my arms and legs in the shot. How to make the right sounds." He grinned. "How to say 'Fuck yeah' a lot. I started working out, bulking up a little. Except the studio I was with at the time had something to say about that. They told me an over-muscled body looks fat on camera, and to aim for deep definition, which doesn't look too muscular." He snorted. "Then I overhauled my diet. I took out all the chemicals, excess sodium, sugar…"

"I never knew looking good could be such hard work."

"The thing is, once you get into shape? You have to stay that way. *That's* the hard work. And as my body shape changed, so did my audience."

Dylan's cheeks were flushed. "Now you come to mention it… yeah, you do say fuck yeah a lot."

He laughed. "You know what's weird? If you watch vintage porn—and by that, I mean stuff produced in the sixties or seventies—there wasn't all that much talking. Now?" He waggled his eyebrows.

"Dirty talk is hot. There's always plenty of noise."

"I see what you mean about changes."

Mark shook his head. "That's not what I meant. Studios started to close, due to pressure and falling subscriptions."

"What kind of pressure?"

"Sex is a dirty word, didn't you know that? And gone are the days when people subscribed to watch your latest video. *Now* you can simply go to a gay porn site and see whatever you want for free. I started working for myself. I get to decide what content I make, how often I put out videos. Except I still run into that same problem—folks who think I shouldn't make money for what I do, so they upload my stuff to those aforementioned sites. I did work as an escort, until they started closing those sites down too. And don't get me started on what the government is doing to sex workers."

Dylan's brow furrowed. "You said it was never going to be long-term—maybe it's time for a career rethink?"

"I've thought about it, believe me." Mark took a deep breath. "I didn't invite you here to listen to me bitch and moan about my woes, so let's change the subject."

"I don't mind, honest." Dylan's gaze was earnest. "I kinda get the feeling you needed to get stuff off your chest. I'm good at listening."

"Does it come with the territory?" Mark inquired.

Dylan's eyes gleamed. "You learn to nod in all the right places."

He guffawed. "It's like that, is it? Okay, got any ideas where you'd like to take me?"

"One at the moment, but it's a bit different. It's also more of a fun day, rather than sightseeing."

Mark huffed. "Fun? What's that? I'd be up for that." Dylan had already brought a breath of fresh air into Mark's life.

Dylan glanced at the clock on the wall. "I'd better be going. I'm on early tomorrow, and it promises to be another busy day."

Mark got out his phone and scrolled to Contacts. He handed it over. "Here. Put your number in there. We'll talk Monday night to arrange a time to meet up. Now, about this walk… Am I going to need hiking gear?"

Dylan laughed. "It's a gentle stroll. Now, if you really want to do some serious hiking, I'd be up for that too. There are loads of great hikes we could do, but we'd have to make an early start."

Mark smiled. "I'm going to put myself entirely in your hands."

What surprised him was how much the prospect warmed —and delighted—him.

Dylan got up. "Thanks for the coffee—and thanks again for being so understanding about… you know."

"Forgiven and forgotten, okay?" Mark walked him to the door. "I'll see you Tuesday. I hope the next couple of days aren't too hectic."

Dylan sighed. "Once Labor Day has come and gone, it'll be full steam ahead into Halloween." He held out his hand, and Mark shook it. "Till Tuesday."

Mark watched him as he strolled along Acorn Drive. When he reached the road, Dylan turned and waved, then headed left. Mark closed the door and bolted it.

A really nice guy.

There was only one thing wrong with Dylan—he was straight. At least, he insisted he wasn't gay, despite admitting to watching Mark's videos. A line from Shakespeare flitted through his mind, and for a dude who'd been dead for over four hundred years, he pretty much nailed it.

The lady doth protest too much, methinks.

Okay, so Dylan was no lady, but the rest of it was on the money. Mark was still trying to figure how *straight* Dylan really was.

Chapter Seven

September 7

The house was quiet, but that was only because Steve was still asleep, Dawson had gotten the weekend off to visit his folks—and Dylan longed to know how he'd managed to pull *that* off, apart from selling his soul, of course. Greg wasn't home from working the night shift yet. Dylan was grateful for the peaceful start to the day, because once he ambled into the hotel, it would be nonstop until he was done.

At least I get to relax tomorrow. He was looking forward to the early morning stroll with Mark. The Marginal Way was Dylan's favorite walk, especially first thing in the morning. Sharing it with Mark was a bonus.

This still feels a little surreal. One minute, Mark was a naked guy on a screen—a guy Dylan would *never* own up to following—and the next, he was a warm, genuine man in need of… company? Friendship? The request to show Mark around had certainly come across as genuine, and once he'd gotten over his initial misgivings, Dylan couldn't see any harm in agreeing to his suggestion.

His phone buzzed, and he hoped it wasn't work. When he saw Seb's name, he laughed out loud. As soon as the call connected, Dylan burst out, "Since when do you get up this early on a holiday?"

"Okay, wise guy, so you know me. And the answer is, since Marcus's family descended on him for the weekend. It's been almost as hectic as the Fourth was. Not as many people, thank God, but enough that it's not quiet around here. And calling you wasn't my idea. This is down to Marcus." Dylan heard yelling in the background, and Seb groaned. "Okay, okay, I'm coming. Here, *you* wanted to talk to him—take the phone, while I go see what your mom wants. Dylan? Later."

Dylan chuckled. Seb sounded as if he was already part of the family.

"Hey, how are you?" Marcus came across as a whole lot calmer than Seb.

"Doing okay. Busy, of course, but that's to be expected. I'm due at the hotel in an hour." Dylan caught more raised voices. "Sounds as if you have your hands full."

"In more ways than one."

That had an ominous ring to it. "Everything okay?"

"Remember I told you I have a nephew? The one I was handing out advice to this summer?"

"Sure."

"Well, the last time he was here, I knew something wasn't right. I'm still no clearer, but last night he asked if he could come visit me again when the rest of the family had left. He says he needs to talk to me."

"That sounds... serious."

Marcus sighed. "That's what I thought too. And it got me to thinking about you. So... how are you, apart from work keeping you busy?"

Warmth spread through Dylan's chest.

"Thanks for asking. I'm okay."

"And how's that manager treating you?"

"He's... he's okay too."

"Do I hear a little hesitation?"

It took Dylan about a heartbeat to decide to come clean. Marcus was one of the good guys, of that he was certain. "Remember when we all went to the beach, and I told you about that porn star who'd been filming in the hotel?"

"The problem you needed to solve? Yes, I remember."

"Well... he came back."

There was silence for a moment, and when Marcus spoke, Dylan could hear the smile in his voice. "'He'?"

Oh shit.

"Keeping track of pronouns can be a bitch, right? And it's a wise man who can remember when he's changed someone's gender accidentally on purpose." Before Dylan could respond, Marcus continued. "It's all right, I won't say a word to Seb. So... I gather you like this guy's... work?"

"Well... I..."

"Dylan." Marcus's voice was gentle. "What did I say to you, the night we met? It's okay to be curious. If you need to talk, you know where I am. And if you need to move beyond curiosity, that's okay too."

Except there was more than curiosity at work—there were desires Dylan didn't want *anyone* to know about, especially his friends. Because he didn't think he could tell them what he really wanted, not without shame washing over him, so much shame he'd probably drown in it.

"Thanks, Marcus. And if I ever do need to

talk…"

"I should let you go about your day. I hope you're not exhausted by the end of it. But there *is* something I'd like to know."

"Yeah?"

"This porn star who returned to the hotel… what happened?"

"His shoot was a bust. Someone told the manager what was going down, and he was asked to leave the hotel."

Another bout of silence. "That was you, wasn't it?"

"How did you—"

"Intuition."

Dylan expelled a breath. "My hand was kinda forced. And now I'm trying to make amends."

"Color me intrigued."

"Well, he wants to get to know this part of Maine, so… I've agreed to act as a… guide."

Marcus whistled. "Nice. What's his name? I might have seen his videos."

"Mark Roman." Dylan swore he caught Marcus's sharp intake of breath. "Marcus?"

"Damn. You have excellent taste. I'm green with envy." He chuckled. "Except what would I do with a gorgeous porn star? I have enough on my plate dealing with Seb. And you did *not* hear me say that, all right?"

Dylan laughed. "You forget. I *know* Seb." The sound of the door slamming shut brought him back into the present with a bang. "I gotta go."

"Enjoy your stint as a tour guide. I just hope he's a nice guy."

"He is." Dylan only had one evening of dinner

and coffee to go on, but his instincts told him Mark wouldn't treat him badly. "And I hope whatever's going on with your nephew isn't too serious."

"Thank you for that. I hope to see you soon. And Dylan?" Marcus cleared his throat. "If you want to bring Mark over for a visit…"

Dylan guffawed as he disconnected the call. Marcus had nailed it. Mark *was* gorgeous. *And Mark thinks I'm good-looking.*

He pushed the thought aside. *Don't go getting ideas. He just wants a friend.* And besides, how many times had Dylan reiterated that he wasn't gay?

Then he sighed. *Why should Mark believe that, when I'm not even sure I do anymore?*

By the time Mark had hopped around the channels maybe three or four times, he gave in to his first instinct and turned off the TV. There were unread books on the shelf and the coffee table, books he'd bought because they'd sounded interesting, but he was in no mood to read. He was up-to-date with his videos—if anything he was long overdue to upload another—and he hated the idea of doing another round of social media promo.

I really am getting sick of this. Dylan's words from Saturday night were suddenly right there, front and center.

"Maybe it's time for a career change?"

Which sounded like the perfect solution, except for one thorny issue—what the fuck would he do to keep body and soul together? He had no qualifications to fall back on, and while seventeen years in the porn industry was impressive, and had proved lucrative on occasions, it didn't exactly look good on a résumé.

His phone buzzed, and Mark deliberated answering when he saw Joey's name. Joey only ever called for one reason. He waited until the rings stopped, not surprised by the notification of voice mail.

"Hey, Mark. You doing anything this Saturday? Only, I'll be in New York, and I thought we might meet up."

Meet up. Yeah, right. That was Joey-speak for *let's shoot some porn.*

"Anyhow, call me when you get this. I'm staying in Brooklyn with a friend, Chaz, and he says we can use his place. He might even join us, if we're real lucky. He's fucking hot, by the way. He's dipping his toes into porn, and I think he'd be a real draw. Call me, okay? It's been too long."

Mark exited the voice mail and tossed his phone onto the couch beside him. He didn't really have an excuse to turn Joey down, and he hadn't uploaded anything for a couple of weeks. Plus, there were any number of guys who'd jump at the chance to film with him. New York was beginning to sound like a good idea, especially if he could spend a couple of days there and get enough content to last him a while.

Decision made.

Mark clicked on Joey's number. "Hey. Sorry, I

couldn't get to the phone."

"Sure. I thought you might be …busy, y'know? So… whadaya think?"

"I like. I just need to make some calls, set up more shoots."

"Gotcha. I get in Friday morning, so if you wanna drive down and stay Friday night, Chaz says you can have the couch. Yeah, I already asked. I had a feeling you'd bite." Joey snickered. "Not seen all that much of you lately. And I heard about last weekend. Austin called. Bummer."

Mark snorted. "The porn grapevine has been busy, I see. Yeah, I need to put some stuff out there."

"Great. We can shoot over the weekend. And if I find more guys who want in, I'll let you know. Been a while since either of us shot a gangbang. You up for that?"

Not in the slightest. Except he knew when push came to shove, he'd put on a good show for the cameras. He'd been at this business long enough to fake it with the best of them.

Might have to take some little blue pills along as backup, just in case. If Chaz was as hot as Joey said, getting it up wouldn't be all that difficult. The only difficulty he could envisage was shooting with a complete novice, but if they talked it through enough on Friday night, that might make things easier.

"Mark? You still there?"

He gave himself a mental shake. "Yeah, I'm here. See what you can do, I'll go along with it."

"Great. I *might* have mentioned I was thinking of asking you, and I've got a list of guys who are already drooling. There are these three twinks who wanna fuck a daddy. Might be right up your street."

Joey chuckled. "You might even get all three dicks in your ass. *That* would get your site noticed." Another wry chuckle. "DILFs are hot right now."

Mark had had enough. "Text me the address, and where I can park, and I'll see you Friday. Thanks, Joey." He disconnected before Joey could continue, then gazed at his surroundings. Forget the TV and books: the solution to his present situation of *what to do?* was obvious—shoot some content.

Mark closed the blinds, then set up a couple of tripods and lights. He placed one at the end of the couch and one on the coffee table. Then he undid his jeans and tugged on his cock until he was hard.

Time to perform.

He started the camera on his phone and tablet, then reclined on the couch on the towel he'd laid out, his zipper lowered, revealing his tight pubes. Without a glance at either camera, Mark reached into his jeans and stroked his dick.

"It's been a while since I bust a nut for ya," he said in a low voice. "So this might not last long. We'll see." He freed his shaft, tugging on it, rolling his hips as he slid his hand along its length. It wasn't long before the jeans had been discarded, the tee removed, and he was naked, one hand wrapped around his cock while he fingered his hole. He didn't talk—that wasn't his style with solos—but his soft sighs and low moans were audible. He knelt over the couch, his head on a pile of cushions, his back to the coffee table, and spread his legs, watching the screen through them as he played with his ass and gave his dick slow tugs. Then it was onto his back, legs drawn up to his chest as he worked his shaft, occasionally rubbing his balls and taint before moving lower to tease his hole with the pad of his finger.

Mark was on autopilot, his mind drifting through a series of rooms in his head, containing recollections of heated moments. What shocked him was a new room, with only one occupant.

Mark caught his breath as Dylan stood at the foot of a wide bed, his black shirt open at the neck, his waistcoat unbuttoned, and an obvious bulge in his pants.

"You want this?" Mark stroked a single finger over his hole.

Dylan didn't respond, his gaze locked on Mark's ass, his lips parted.

"Come closer. I want to feel your breath here." He spread his ass cheeks, stretching his hole, and Dylan's breathing hitched. "You ever eaten ass before?"

Dylan shook his head.

"Want to?"

Dylan shuddered. "I…" He licked his lips.

"Take off your clothes, Dylan. Show me what you look like under that uniform." Mark tugged gently on his dick as Dylan removed his clothing with trembling hands. As he unfastened his pants and pulled on the zipper, Mark couldn't tear his eyes away from the rigid shaft that bobbed up as Dylan pushed his pants and underwear past his hips. "Fuck. That's a pretty cock." It was long and slender, with a wide head that Mark bet would feel amazing as it penetrated him. Dylan was just perfect: a hairy chest, not too much, and a trail of fuzz leading down to his crotch. Pointy little nips begging to be sucked, flicked, bitten… A lean torso that Mark wanted to kiss and lick…

He didn't want to wait a second longer.

Mark squeezed lube onto his fingers, then slid two into his ass, his hips moving as he prepped his hole for Dylan's cock. "Fuck me," he whispered. "You know you want to. You don't have to hold back anymore. Take my hole. It's yours."

Dylan swallowed. He got onto the bed and grabbed Mark's ankles, spreading him wide, his dick jutting out, leaking pre-cum in a glistening thread.

Mark nodded as he reached for Dylan's shaft, guiding it into position. "In me, please." He could feel its heat pressing against his slick pucker. "Dylan…"

With a groan, Dylan pushed…

And Mark shot over his abs and chest, unable to hold it back. He groaned as he came, his body shaking with each drop that pulsed from the slit. He squeezed his dick, working it until he was spent, then expelled a breath.

"Fuck…"

Mark got up from the couch and switched off the cameras, then flopped back onto the towel.

Okay, where did that come from? He closed his eyes, but Dylan was gone, leaving only the memory of a firm body that Mark hadn't gotten the chance to feel against his skin.

Talk about an overactive imagination. And since when did Mark fantasize about straight guys? Because that was all it could be—the fantasy of coaxing Dylan to fuck him. He'd better push such thoughts out of his head before he met up with Dylan in the morning.

Explaining why he had a hard-on might prove a little difficult.

Chapter Eight

September 8

Mark locked the car and scanned the parking lot for any sign of Dylan. The promise of a great breakfast at the end of the walk had been enough for him to make do with coffee and an apple bran muffin. Dylan had sent him the menu for the café where they'd be heading, and Mark was already salivating at the prospect of an omelet filled with ham, bacon, sausage, pepper, onion and cheddar.

Don't eat too much. You don't want to pile on the pounds before Friday.

Sometimes Mark hated watching his diet. He could almost believe carbs lay in wait for him around every corner, ready to tempt him with pizza, pasta smothered in a rich sauce, crispy fries that cried out to be dipped in garlic mayo…

Christ, I must be hungrier than I thought.

The sun had been up about two hours, and it looked as if it would be a beautiful day. The temperature was pleasant and the air was still.

"Morning."

Mark jumped and spun around. Dylan stood there with a smile, dressed in blue cargo shorts, a paler blue tee, and white sneakers. He carried a small backpack over his left shoulder, and sunglasses hid his eyes. Mark returned his smile. "Hey. Looks like we picked the right day for a walk. Where does it start?"

Dylan pointed to the road at the end of Cottage Street. "We go along Shore Road for one block, then turn left. The Way actually begins at Shore Road." He gazed at the sky. "You're right. It's a gorgeous day. Ready?"

Mark nodded, and they walked out of the lot, heading for the road. When they took a left, the ocean lay before them, a dark blue strip meeting the cloudless sky at the horizon, dotted here and there with sails. "Have you ever done that?" He pointed to a boat.

Dylan laughed. "Hell no. When I was fourteen, my family took me on a cruise to Monhegan Island to see the lighthouse, and watch for puffins and seals. I think I threw up the whole time we were on the ferry."

"Yeah, something tells me you're definitely a landlubber. Can't say I'm a fan of sailing either. I prefer to keep my feet on solid ground." They reached the ocean, and spread before them was a sandy beach, mostly obscured by rocks and pebbles. The tide was out, and the sun sparkled on the water. Railings stood on both sides of the path, and on their right was a large hotel fronted by neatly mowed lawns, littered with loungers and parasols.

"That's where you stay if you want a view," Dylan murmured. He gestured to the railing. "I think that's to keep out the riffraff."

Mark inhaled deeply. "It's so peaceful here." The fence leaned in places, struggling against the shrubs and undergrowth threatening its stability. The path followed the graceful curve of the land, and as they rounded the corner, he spied a bench overlooking a small cove. Trees overhung the path, and a wooden walkway led down to the sand.

"That's Little Beach." Dylan pointed to the cove, then to the rocky headland. "And that's Israel Head."

"Why is it called that?"

Dylan shrugged. "No clue. I do know it was named in the original land sale, back in 1925. Some guy called Josiah Chase retired to York, and bought twenty acres from Perkins Cove to here. The Way was only a mile long, but since he died, people have contributed pockets of land, and extended it by maybe a quarter of a mile."

Mark chuckled. "Did you swallow a guide book this morning? Or are you always this knowledgeable?"

"You nailed it the other night. Giving out tourist info is part of my job. And I should know all this after eight years." He gestured to the path. "It's survived a couple of wicked bad storms over the years, so much so that they set up an Endowment Fund to preserve and protect it from the weather—and the countless visitors." He paused at a bench. "Mind if we stop? I know we've only just started, but there are benches all the way along here, and I like to sit and gaze at the ocean."

"I think that sounds the perfect way to make the walk last a little longer." Mark was in no hurry to get home, although his stomach was just beginning to complain that someone had apparently cut his throat.

They sat on the wooden slats, and Mark leaned back. He caught a scent on the slight breeze, and sniffed. "Oh wow. That's heavenly."

"Honeysuckle." Dylan smiled. "I love that smell."

"Me too. It reminds me of my grandparents' place. The back yard fence between it and the house next door was covered in the stuff. I could smell it in my bedroom." A breeze came off the ocean, hitting him square in the face, and it was exhilarating.

"Where did you live in Wyoming?"

"Cheyenne." Mark snorted. "As far removed from Wells as it's possible to get. I couldn't wait to leave there." Except that wasn't entirely true. He hadn't minded his hometown so much until he'd hit his late teens.

That was when his world had imploded.

"Was it so bad, your life at home?" Dylan asked in a low voice. Before Mark could respond, he held up his hands. "Hey, you know what? You don't have to answer that. It's none of my business."

Mark had been out of their clutches long enough that he could speak about it dispassionately—most of the time. There were still days when he'd recall words spoken in the heat of the moment, and his guts would twist.

"It's okay. I can talk about it." *And when was the last time I did that?*

Dylan removed a bottle of water from his backpack and took a drink before holding it out to Mark. "Want some?"

Mark nodded and drank a few mouthfuls. He handed the bottle back, and gazed out at the serene scene, inhaling the mingled aromas of honeysuckle and wild roses. "When I was a kid, I loved spending time with my family. I have two brothers and one sister—I'm the baby of the family." Except he didn't have brothers or a sister anymore—they'd told him so, the day he'd left.

"Me too."

He smiled. "It was great. They were always looking out for me, you know? And my parents... A guy never had better."

"Based on what you said on Saturday, I'm guessing that changed."

Mark huffed. "In a heartbeat. I'd always thought they'd support me, no matter what. Turns out, there was only one thing we disagreed on, and it was a deal-breaker."

"Was this when you came out to them?" Dylan asked, his voice low.

Mark rolled out a heavy sigh. "Not exactly. I was seventeen, about to graduate high school... and I thought I was in love. Head over heels, totally smitten, in love. Of course, it wasn't love, just a first crush, and the guy on the receiving end of all this adoration didn't have a fucking clue. So... I came to a decision. I was going to tell him how I felt, which, looking back, was the stupidest thing in the *history* of stupid things."

"Why do I get the feeling I'm about to say 'ouch'?"

Mark smiled. "Because you've heard this story before. I waited till after gym class, which was the last class on a Friday, and then I asked him if we could go someplace to talk. He said yes—he was a nice guy—but when I finally managed to stammer out how I felt..." He swallowed. Kevin's face could have been carved out of stone. "He told me he could never think of me like that. And then he told me we were never to mention it again." Mark gestured to the bottle. "Could I...?"

"Sure." Dylan handed it over, and Mark drank a little more, as much as his tight throat would allow.

He wiped his mouth. "We're talking a couple of weeks before graduation. So yeah, it hurt to have him react like that, but I thought... I can survive a few weeks. After that, I'd probably never see him again, right?" He shivered. "Only... that night, my dad got a call from Kevin's dad. My dad called me into the kitchen, told me to sit, and then shut the door."

"You can stop right there. I think I know the rest." Dylan's eyes were warm. "What happened then?"

"Well... there was a visit from our pastor. I don't think you need three guesses to know what *he* said. And then my parents kept repeating everything he'd come out with, endlessly, until I wanted to scream. This went on all freaking summer. I'd go out, just to get away from them, but as soon as my feet crossed that threshold, it would start all over again. "

"Had there been any clues that was how they felt?"

Mark shook his head. "They'd never talked about their opinions. If they had, I'd have thought twice about the whole Kevin episode, in case it got back to them. No, that was a bolt from the blue. What twisted the knife even more? My brothers and sister got in on the act. My oldest brother was a little more blunt than my parents. He told me there was no way he was having a fag for a brother." He could still see Paul's face, reddened and contorted with disgust.

"What was the last straw? What made you decide to walk out of there?"

"They brought up the subject of college. They said they weren't going to pay for my tuition if I carried on with this... 'perversion'," he air-quoted. Mark stared out at the calm waters of the Atlantic.

"They left that part till the last minute. I mean, I was already packing." His chest was as tight as a drum. "I could've caved. I could've agreed, and said you know what? You're right. I'm not gay. And everything would've been rosy. Except it wouldn't. Because while I could live the way I wanted in college, away from their eyes, what about when I came home? What about the rest of my fucking *life*? I couldn't live like that. Because who wants to hide what they truly are?"

Jesus, it still burned.

"And that was when you left?"

Mark nodded. "A few days after my eighteenth birthday. I called them from the bus station, and told them why I'd left. I didn't tell them where I was headed. Turned out, they didn't care. They didn't want to know."

"And Mark Roman was born." Dylan cocked his head. "I'm assuming that isn't your real name."

"It is now. I don't want the one they gave me."

Dylan's eyes widened. "*Now* I understand about your grandparents. Your grandmother felt the same as your parents, didn't she? But your grandfather didn't. And that's why he got in touch after she died, to make sure you knew he still loved you."

Mark was touched Dylan had remembered the details of their conversation. "Yeah. Grandpa is awesome." He cleared his throat. "Can we walk some more?" The trip down Memory Lane made his chest ache and his stomach clench. *I guess I haven't forgotten entirely.*

The recollections still hurt like a son of a bitch.

"Sure." They got up from the bench, and Dylan pointed to the left. "That's Israel Head Road, but we continue this way, sticking to the coast."

Mark loved the sight of roofs peeking above treetops, a mix of green and white. Now and then they'd encounter people coming from the opposite direction, walking briskly, earbuds in, or jogging. At one location a mini lighthouse had been constructed in the middle of the path, a cute touch. Houses stood on the right, their porches facing the ocean, and numerous paths led from the concreted Way down to the beach. Benches sat at regular intervals, and on one a man gazed out at the view.

Mark could understand why. The serenity of the landscape, the wind in the trees, the sound of the waves... Perfect.

When they reached a bronze plaque giving details about Josiah Chase, Mark couldn't resist. "Hey, look at that. You got the date right and everything." That earned him an eye-roll.

They passed through a set of stone gateposts, followed by a bridge that crossed a stream wending its way to the ocean. The shoreline became more defined, with layers of rock, broken here and there by trees. A spit of land protruded in the distance, covered with buildings.

Dylan paused at another viewpoint. "I just want to drink this all in."

Mark stood and took in the water rippling over the rocks, and the *caw* of crows circling above their heads. "I can see why you like this walk."

"I always stop here, because after this point we reach civilization." He inclined his head toward the spit. "That's Perkins Cove. We're almost at the end of the way."

Mark grinned. "Does that mean brunch?"

Dylan laughed. "Yeah, it does. I just want to

enjoy this a while longer." He inclined his head toward yet another bench. "That okay?"

Mark smiled. "More than okay."

They sat with the sun on their faces. Mark couldn't remember the last time he'd felt so relaxed. "So how civilized is Perkins Cove?"

"It's got your usual tourist fare—antique shops, clothing stores, candles... Plus, there's a footbridge that goes across the inlet, and you can stand on it for a great view of the Basin, usually full of boats. The shore is rockier, but there are little coves here and there... Jacks Cove, Rose Cove..." He smiled. "If you like your restaurants with a view, Perkins Cove is the place to be."

"And this place where we're going to eat... what's it like?"

"Cove Café? White cedar shakes, blue-and-white striped awnings, window boxes full of pretty flowers... What it lacks in a view, it makes up for with its menu." He paused. "Thank you, by the way."

"For what?"

"Sharing. You didn't have to tell me all that. And I know you said you can talk about it, but I'll make a guess that it still hurts. Shit has a habit of lingering sometimes."

Mark glanced at Dylan's tight expression. *You're speaking from experience.* He wasn't about to pry— the coals of his past had been raked over enough for one day, and any more would shatter the fragile bubble of time that encapsulated them.

We have time, if he wants to talk. This was only the first such encounter.

His stomach growled, and Dylan guffawed. "I guess that's the end of *that* conversation. Come on, let's feed you." They got up from the bench, and headed along the path bordered on one side by the algae-covered rocky shore, and on the other by guest houses and hotels, all covered in the same gray cedar shakes. As they strolled through the parking lot to join Perkins Cove Road, Mark found himself hoping the day wouldn't end after brunch.

He wanted to hold onto this feeling of peace while he could, before the demands of real life crept in and robbed him of it.

Chapter Nine

September 12

Mark didn't think he had a drop of cum left in him. They'd started filming Saturday afternoon, and so far they had to have shot about four hours of footage. Joey had been right about one thing—Chaz was hot. He was also a fast learner.

Who am I kidding? This guy was made for porn.

He wiped Joey's spunk from his torso, and sagged against the pillows. Chaz seemed a little lost now the cameras had stopped. Joey was busy removing the duct tape from the walls where they'd fastened the phones.

"Was that okay?" Chaz asked, his gaze flitting from Joey to Mark.

Before Mark could respond, Joey snorted. "Are you kidding? You're a natural, kid. You need to think about getting your own site." He grinned. "You've got a future in this."

Mark leveled a hard stare at Joey. "Not *everyone* wants to be a porn star, okay?"

Joey arched his eyebrows. "Maybe he wants to be the next Mark Roman, ever think about that?"

Chaz coughed. "Hey, can I take a piss and grab a shower before you plot out a career for me?"

Mark gave him a sympathetic glance. "You feeling okay?"

Chaz shivered. "To be honest? I'm feeling kinda shaky. I was all kinds of nervous about this, and now that it's over…"

Mark nodded. "I know. I crashed after my first scene. Go shower. Take as long as you like. You'll feel better afterward."

Chaz smiled. "I feel better already." He headed for the bathroom.

When the door closed behind Chaz, Joey gave Mark a speculative glance. "What's with you, Mr. Grumpy?"

"What do you mean? And who's grumpy?"

"You. Don't deny it." Joey snatched the towel from him and wiped himself down. "The kid was okay, wasn't he?"

"He was great," Mark admitted.

"Then what's the problem? And don't tell me there isn't one, because I'll call you a big fucking liar." He sat on the bed. "I'm only asking because… well… you're not yourself."

Mark blinked. "And that's based on your intimate knowledge of me? We've worked together maybe four, five times?" His heart raced. Joey always had been perceptive.

"Yeah, we have. And I've watched every video you've ever been in, so don't tell me I can't tell when your heart isn't in it." He inclined his head toward the bathroom. "Chaz has got a body to die for, a wicked tongue and a dick that doesn't quit. And if all that doesn't rev your engine, there is something seriously wrong."

Mark was on the verge of telling him he was seeing things, until he reconsidered. "I… I think I've had enough."

"Of what, exactly? People paying to watch you fuck?"

"If that's all they did, then I'd be okay. But it's everything else that goes with it." Mark sighed. "The other day, I drove to Portland to do some shopping. I got out of my car and was walking toward the door of the store, when this young guy approached. I knew exactly what he was going to say before he opened his mouth."

"Hey, I know lots of guys who'd kill to have your fan base."

"They can have them," Mark retorted. "And yes, I know it should make me happy that I have so many fans, but I've been doing this for *seventeen freaking years*, and I think that's a long enough stint, don't you? But it's not just the men who want to take a selfie with me, it's the ones who call out my name in the street, who come up to me in a bar and grab my ass, because that's okay, I'm a porn star. It's the constant need to make content so I can eat, pay my bills, buy toilet paper…" He expelled a breath. "This is a sideline for you. When you're not shooting videos, you have a job. This *is* my job. I don't have anything else to fall back on."

Lord, he was tired.

"Maybe you need to take a break," Joey suggested.

"And do what? Visit family? No, thank you. Visit friends?"

Joey said nothing for a moment. "What happened with Dolan? That guy you were seeing a while back?"

"The same thing that happens with every guy I date—he decided he couldn't cope with the idea of me fucking other guys for a living. It *always* gets in the way." Mark stared at him. "I never lie about what I do. I'm always upfront about it. And at the beginning, they all say the same things. 'I don't mind if you have sex with all these men.' 'I think it's hot.' 'It's okay, because you're just fucking them—I know you *love* me.'"

Joey's gaze grew thoughtful. "And did you? Love them, I mean."

Mark took a deep breath. "I came close once, or at least, I thought I did. But as he told me recently, maybe what I *really* loved was the idea someone was in love with me."

"That was Casey, wasn't it? I remember."

Mark grabbed a bottle of water from the nightstand and took a long drink. He wiped his lips. "Casey wants me to fall head over heels. He also wants me to get a life." He gestured to the bed, the phones, the ring lights. "I *have* a life."

He just wasn't sure he liked it all that much anymore.

"What you *don't* have is a work-life balance." Joey's gaze locked on his. "This is all you do, isn't it? Eat, drink, shop, sleep, shoot porn, edit porn, upload porn, promote porn… rinse, repeat…"

"Hey, I'm working on that, all right? I even made a start. I went for a walk."

"Sure you did. And I bet the whole time, you were thinking about who you were gonna shoot with next."

Mark smiled. "Actually? I was distracted from such thoughts by the guy walking beside me."

Joey stilled. "This sounds promising. Who is he?"

"You can stop right there. He's straight. Well… he *says* he's straight. Personally, I think the jury is still out on that one. He's showing me around Maine, that's all." He chuckled. "Okay, so maybe we'll stick to around Wells. The state is freaking *huge*."

"Wait a sec. You said he was a distraction. So… he's good-looking?"

Dylan's face was right there in his head. "Yup. He's also a sweet guy."

Joey grinned. "Okay. Dr. Joey is on the case. Here's my prescription. I recommend spending more time with this guy."

Mark laughed. "Oh yeah? And in the meantime, are you going to buy my groceries? Pay my utility bills?"

"There has to be another way to generate income, apart from the porn." Joey's brow furrowed. "Of course, it doesn't help when guys upload your content to free sites, but that's quickly becoming the norm. It'd be no different if you were working for a studio, right? You'd be making even less money, and your stuff would still get shared."

"Trust me, I've been thinking about alternatives for a while now."

Joey's eyes were warm. "Did you really mean it? When you said you've had enough?"

Mark sighed heavily. "It's getting that way."

"Then maybe you should go out with a bang. Literally." There was that grin again.

"What are you up to?"

"Well… you know those twinks I was telling you about? They couldn't make it this weekend, but they said they'll be free in a few weeks. Wanna shoot an orgy? You, me, the three of them, and anyone else who's interested in being part of Mark Roman's swan song?"

"'Swan song'?" Mark was struggling to keep up. They'd gone from discussing the prospect to making it a reality.

"Put it this way. You got enough saved up so you won't starve?"

He thought for a moment. "Possibly. I could do a lot of solo stuff to bring in a little more."

Joey nodded. "That's the ticket. Morning wood, ass play, ride a dildo, finger-fuck, a little edging…" He grinned. "There ya go. I've just planned out your content for the next two weeks. And I won't even charge you for it."

Mark laughed.

"Guys?" Chaz walked into the bedroom in a towel. "Bathroom's free."

Joey's eyes gleamed, and Mark knew something was coming. "Great. My phone's waterproof, so why don't you film me and Mark having a shower?"

Mark glanced at Joey's cock, which was already rising, and snorted. "You're not talking about me shampooing your head, are you?"

"Shower sex is hot, babe." Joey rubbed his fingers together. "And sex is money."

Mark rolled his eyes. "Fine. Fuck me in the shower." He gave Chaz a mock glare. "You're there to film, not to join in, okay?" He'd seen the size of the tub.

Chaz pouted. "Aw."

He laughed. "You'll get your turn tomorrow, all right? I promise. We'll shoot a morning scene before I drive back to Maine."

That earned him a smile. "Awesome. Can we do a DP?"

Mark laughed his ass off. "Don't run before you can walk, kid."

Joey got off the bed, went over to where his bag sat on the floor, and reached into it. He removed a fat butt plug and slapped it into Chaz's hand. "Don't listen to him. You just need to stretch your hole beforehand." He grinned. "Come on. Time to get wet."

Mark's heart pounded, and his pulse raced. It took him a moment to realize what excited him was not the prospect of Joey fucking his brains out in the shower, or the two of them drilling Chaz's ass.

It was the idea that the end might really be in sight.

I need to make this happen. And in order to do that, he also needed to come up with alternatives— fast.

Dylan walked into the kitchen, the pizza box in his hands. Greg was loading the dishwasher. "About time," Dylan groused. He'd intended reminding Greg it was his turn to clean the kitchen: it looked as if every pot and dish had been used.

"You could've done this yourself, you know," Greg fired back.

"Uh-uh. That's why we have a chores list. I cleaned the bathroom. *You* clean the kitchen."

Greg sniffed. "Ooh. Smells good."

"Yeah, it does, so if you want some…" Dylan grinned. "Either go and find some, or get them to deliver, because you're not having any of mine. I've been thinking about this for the past two hours." He'd finished his shift when Mr. Reynolds had asked him to work reception: Caroline had had to leave early. Dylan couldn't complain—stepping in on demand came with being a supervisor, after all.

"Stingy." Greg's eyes gleamed. "You might wanna eat it with the TV turned up loud."

Dylan groaned. That meant only one thing— Dawson's girlfriend was staying the night. "Seriously?"

Greg nodded. "They've been banging all afternoon. I'm jealous as fuck."

He frowned. "You don't even like Helena."

"Fuck, I don't wanna screw her—I'm in total awe of Dawson's stamina. I mean, *Jesus*…"

Dylan chuckled. "Ah. Boner envy." He put down the box and went to the fridge to grab a soda. Greg inched closer, and Dylan glared. "Nope. Keep your mitts off. Besides, you wouldn't like it."

"It's pizza, what's not to like?"

He grinned. "It has spinach on it. You don't do green stuff."

Greg grimaced. "Yuck. Yeah, you can keep it." He cocked his head to one side. "Has Marie said anything to you?"

Dylan paused, his hands full. "About what?" Marie had started work at the hotel in August, in housekeeping. She seemed okay, not that Dylan had paid her all that much attention.

"Oh, just something I heard, that's all."

Greg's nonchalant air aroused Dylan's suspicious nature. "What? *What* did you hear?"

"She has the hots for you, apparently. She's been asking around if you're dating anyone at the moment." Greg leered. "I think you might have a chance with her. Ask her out."

Dylan gaped at him. "If I want your help arranging a date, I'll ask for it."

"Dude, when was the last time you got laid? Because I think it was sometime back when the earth was cooling."

Dylan rolled his eyes. "And *I* think I have a pizza that's getting cold, so if you'll excuse me…" He left the kitchen and went into the living room. The *thud thud thud* of Dawson's bed against the wall had him reaching for the remote in a heartbeat. When he found an action movie, he stopped. He flopped onto the couch, opened the box, and attacked his pizza with gusto. The movie's car chase scene was punctuated with the odd cry of "God, yes," "There," and "Don't stop."

He concentrated on the screen, doing his best to block out the additional soundtrack emanating from Dawson's room. Greg had been correct: it had been a while since Dylan had gotten laid, but he wasn't likely to forget the experience.

Not in a good way either. His cheeks burned to recall Della's expression, her voice… For weeks after, he'd been on tenterhooks, certain she was going to tell all her coworkers about him, his suggestion… He'd walked through the hotel, imagining staff were talking about him, whispering behind his back. When nothing happened, he'd realized she was probably as embarrassed by the episode as he had been.

Avoiding such situations was the way to go. He didn't need anyone else telling him he was a pervert. So what if he was frustrated? Better that than the alternatives.

Marcus's words taunted him. *Explore. Dream. Discover.* Dylan had the dream part down—he wasn't sure he had enough courage for the other two.

Chapter Ten

September 15

It had been a long day, and Dylan was looking forward to finishing his shift and going home. When his phone buzzed, he thought for one awful moment it was Mr. Reynolds calling to ask him to work a few more hours. Then he chuckled.

Idiot. He'd call the office phone, not my cell. Dylan removed it from his pocket, and his stomach clenched when he saw it was a text from his dad.

Call me.

He was tempted to ignore it, but he knew from experience his dad would keep on sending messages until Dylan responded. *Better get it over and done with.*

He clicked on Call, and after five or six rings, his dad answered. "I wasn't sure if you were working. We don't know what your hours are."

Dylan automatically translated that last remark: *You haven't shared your schedule with us.* "I'm done for the day. What's up?"

"Your mom was saying it's been a while since you've visited. Of course, we know how busy you get at the hotel."

Dylan ignored that last bit. "Is she okay?"

"She's fine. You'd know that, if you'd been here in the last month. But it's her birthday soon, and I wanted to make sure you remembered."

Christ, he'd been ten years old, and his mom's birthday had coincided with a school trip to Acadia. *I forgot one freaking time, Dad.* Except he knew there was no point bringing that up. It wouldn't make any difference.

"Yes, it's on my calendar, just like it is every year. Are you planning anything special, seeing as it's a big one?" *See Dad? I do know.*

"I've been discussing it with your sisters, and we've decided to throw her a surprise party."

And I don't get a vote. Not that this was news. "Can I do anything?"

"Well, it's not as if you can do much. You obviously have a lot to do at the hotel. I'll send you the details. I just wanted to give you a heads up so you could schedule it."

"I'll do that." His pulse quickened. *Are we done now?*

"We hardly see you these days."

Wasn't that the general idea? Dylan could still recall the conversation with his dad not long after he'd started at the hotel. The gist of it was that since he was earning, when did he intend moving out? Dylan had had it with the duty visits. They only made him feel useless and anxious. *It doesn't matter what I do. It's never good enough.*

"We're only a small hotel, Dad. There's a lot to do here. And now that I'm a supervisor…"

"Yeah, you mentioned that your last visit."

And you could've said something about that. Maybe, you were proud of me? Yeah right.

"I bet you still find time to see those friends of yours."

Jesus, he fucking *knew* his dad would mention

them. "Not really. I saw them a few months ago at a birthday party." He wasn't going to say a word about Aaron's BBQ.

"I don't suppose they've changed."

"Dad... we talked about this." Dylan wasn't sure why he was wasting his breath.

"I just don't think it's healthy, spending so much time with them. When you were a kid, I was always worried you'd turn out like some of them."

And that was your only concession to me staying friends with them, wasn't it? Dylan could still hear his parents' words.

'As long as you're not one of... them.'

"Sorry, Dad. The manager wants a word with me," he lied. "Gotta go. Let me know when you want me there for the party, and if there's anything I can do." He disconnected, his hand shaking. What upset him most was that he meant that last comment. Years of people-pleasing was a hard habit to shake.

As usual, the conversation left a bitter taste, and Dylan knew it had soured his mood for the evening. What he badly needed was a distraction.

Dylan scrolled to Mark's number and clicked *Call*. When it went to voice mail, he sighed. *Damn it.* "Hey, Mark. Dylan here. Are you doing anything Thursday? I have an idea, if you want to do something different and fun. Call me when you get this." Then he went online to check the opening times, smiling to himself.

It might not be Mark's idea of fun, but then again...

He stared at the phone. *Who am I kidding? It's not the prospect of a fun day out that appeals to me—it's the idea of spending it with Mark.*

September 17

Mark locked his front door. "So, why the mystery? Why can't I know where we're going?"

"It's a surprise." Dylan got into the passenger side.

"Can I at least ask if we're going far?" Dylan had given nothing away in his call.

Dylan chuckled. "Oh yeah, miles. Just follow my directions." He fastened his seatbelt. "I did my homework. This place has been open thirty years, so for all I know, you've probably been there when you were a kid on vacation."

"I can't answer that, now can I, seeing as I have no clue where you're taking me." Mark was enjoying the mystery element.

"Follow signs for Moody. That's all you're getting for now."

He frowned. "That's just down the road from Wells."

"Why yes, it is." Judging by Dylan's smile, he was enjoying himself too.

They'd driven south maybe five minutes when Dylan pointed to a signpost on the right. "We're here."

Mark stared. "Wonder Mountain Fun Park?" The name rang a bell. He turned the car into the parking lot, drove into a space, then switched off the engine. He twisted in his seat to gaze at Dylan. "Isn't this for kids?"

"It's for all ages. Trust me. I came here one summer with my friends, and we had an awesome time."

"And how old were you all at the time?"

Dylan grinned. "In our early twenties." He got out of the car, and Mark did the same. "Look, we could've done some sightseeing along the coast, but I thought no, let's do this instead. I don't know about you, but I want to let loose and have fun."

Mark couldn't remember the last time he'd done that. "So what are we going to do first?"

Dylan pointed to the signpost. "How about Go-karts? A friendly race around the track?"

Mark laughed. "I'm beginning to see what a big kid you are."

"Do any of us ever really grow up?" Dylan cocked his head. "*Did* you come here as a child?"

Mark shook his head. "Not that I recall. I think we drove past here more than once, but we never stopped." Although he did have a vague recollection of asking his dad if they could. "I take it you did."

Dylan nodded. "Every summer. My sisters weren't into go-karts though, and I had to go in the same kart as my mom or dad. Neither of them liked speed much." He gave Mark an obviously hopeful glance.

This was shaping up to be a good day.

The Snake Pit track lived up to its name. Seven hundred feet of banked curves and elevation changes made for an exhilarating ride. Mark had chosen a red kart, and Dylan was in an orange one. They started out slowly, but soon sped up, and from then on it was a race. Dylan's whoops and hollers were a sheer delight, and Mark relished the thrill of the chase, overtaking him on wide bends, yelling when Dylan pulled ahead of him, laughing. Mark forgot his cares and lost himself in the thrill of it all.

Letting go was wonderful.

Adventure Mini-golf was more sedate, but the rivalry continued as they both kept score, amid even more laughter. The Human Maze was a laugh a minute, and Mark got lost more than once. Franky's Game Room turned out to be an arcade with slot machines, claw machines, and one hi-tech variation on Whack-a-mole. Speed of Light was a game for two, with a board filled with lights. The objective was to hit each light that came on, thus bumping up the score, and Dylan proved to be as competitive as Mark. Both of them were laughing their heads off as they attempted to keep up with the lights, and Dylan won by a mere two points.

By the time they'd completed three rounds, Mark was starving.

They bought burgers, fries and sodas from the

concession stand, and sat at wooden tables to eat. All around were families, kids yelling and running around, their parents admonishing them and trying to get them to sit still for a moment. Here and there, Mark spied a couple of teenagers, but as far as he could tell, he and Dylan were the only same-sex couple.

Except we're not a couple, remember? Mark found it difficult to believe he'd known Dylan such a short time. *He's easy to talk to.* That might have accounted for the conversation they'd had while they'd strolled to Perkins Cove the previous week. Sure, it was easier talking to a stranger, but it felt like more than that. In a matter of weeks, Dylan had become a friend.

Mark couldn't stop smiling. "This was a great idea. Thank you."

"You're welcome. I haven't laughed so much in ages. But you make it sound like we're done. There's still more to come." Dylan grinned. "We have Mountain Mania and Nautical Nightmare left." His stomach growled, and he blushed. "After we've eaten."

Mark helped himself to fries. "You must have had a great childhood." He kicked himself when Dylan's face tightened. "I'm sorry. You don't like to talk about it."

"It's okay. In fact, compared to the lives of some of my friends, I had it good growing up." He drank a little from his soda bottle. "I bet if I told you about my family, you'd think 'Why the hell is he making such a big deal out of it?'"

"I wouldn't say that," Mark assured him. "It's all about perspective, right?"

Dylan studied him for a moment. "You're right. The thing is, I... I'm a very private person.

Always have been."

"But you shared stuff with your friends, didn't you?"

Dylan shook his head. "Keeping everything to myself has been a lifelong habit, one that I guess is hard to shake."

"You don't have to talk about it," Mark said earnestly. "I mean it. Don't let it stress you out."

"Maybe bottling it all up is what's stressed me out. Maybe I *should* talk about it." He glanced at his burger and fries. "I think I just lost my appetite."

"If you don't want to eat it, then don't force yourself. I'll buy you something when you feel hungry." Mark was more concerned with whatever was eating away at Dylan.

He pushed his food away. "When I was a kid, my friends… they were my lifeline. They accepted me. They cared for me. I… I was like a sponge, absorbing their friendship. But I couldn't give anything back. My friend, Levi… his grandmother kind of adopted us. We were always welcome there. Only thing was, I couldn't return the invitation."

"Why not?"

Dylan's gaze met his. "Seb used to talk about his mom, how she couldn't accept him being gay. Finn had an equally hard time with his family. My concerns seemed so… feeble next to theirs, so I never talked about them." He gestured to his jeans and tee. "This isn't me. You have *no* idea."

"What do you mean?"

"This is a really relaxed look for me. My friends tease me about being neat all the time, but they don't understand. It's not a conscious decision, it's more that… well, it's *ingrained* in me. I was raised to dress correctly."

"There's nothing wrong with being neat," Mark told him. "We have way too many slobs in the world." He smiled.

Dylan's smile didn't reach his eyes. "If I picked out a T-shirt to wear, one of my parents would say that of course it was my choice, but then they'd mention how my clothing reflected on *them*. If I did well in school, they'd mention how I was *almost* as good as one of my sisters."

"Wow. Talk about passive-aggressive." Mark stilled. "I'm sorry. I shouldn't have said that. It was rude."

Dylan stared at him. "For God's sake, don't apologize. I thought the same thing for years now, only… I wasn't sure if I was reading them all wrong." He swallowed. "For most of my life, I did whatever they wanted, I tried to please them, but it felt as if nothing I did was ever good enough. It's taken me years to realize I can never make them happy." He shivered.

"I think you needed to get that out." Mark couldn't help himself. He reached across the table and took Dylan's hand in his. "There's a term for what your parents put you through, and maybe now you're in the right head space to accept it."

"What term?"

"Emotional abuse."

Dylan's heart fluttered, and his adrenaline spiked, sending shudders coursing through him. In their wake came a wave of peace that lifted him, body and soul. He raised his head high and breathed deeply, his chest free of its invisible constrictions. "I couldn't tell my friends any of this, because that would've meant telling them the rest."

Mark stroked his hand. "It's okay."

Dylan focused on the gentle trace of Mark's fingers, the warm, soothing quality of his voice. "I always felt as if I was a hanger-on. They accepted me, but they knew nothing about my life. When I was fifteen, my parents started voicing their opinions of Seb, Finn, Levi… They didn't want me to stay friends with them."

"Why those three?"

Dylan stared at the wooden tabletop. "They're gay. And in all the years I lived under my parents' roof, there was only ever one thing I refused to do—and that was to give up my friends. I couldn't. I needed them. God, they have no clue just how much."

"How did your parents react?"

He removed his hand from Mark's grasp and met his gaze. "I think you probably know. And when their words didn't work, they made a concession. I could keep my friends—as long as I wasn't one of *them*." He hooked his fingers in the air.

"Have things improved since you left home?"

Dylan snorted. "Not so you'd notice. They still try to manipulate me all the time. Sometimes I don't think they even know they're doing it."

"That's probably very true." Mark sighed. "Look at us. We both have families who cause us pain. Mine are just more… overt than yours."

"Maybe that's why I feel so comfortable with you," Dylan suggested. "Maybe I sensed... I don't know..."

"A kindred spirit?" Mark suggested.

Dylan smiled. "That's as good a term as any, I suppose." He shuddered out a breath. "Whoa. I feel light-headed."

"It's good to let it all out. There's nothing wrong with being a private person, but now and then, you have to... trust someone with the truth."

The tightness in Dylan's chest returned with a vengeance. *But I haven't told you all my truth.* Except Mark was right.

Maybe it was time he told someone, but this was neither the time nor the place.

"So... was this okay, bringing you here?"

Mark's eyes were bright. "Definitely. You said there's more to come though."

There was—in more ways than one. Dylan wanted an answer to the question that had plagued him for so long, and perhaps Mark was the person to ask.

Is there something wrong with me?

Chapter Eleven

September 21

Mark clicked the upload button, then leaned back. *That's another solo session out there.* He had yet to upload part two of the videos featuring Joey and Chaz, but he was going to wait a few days before doing that. The rest of the evening stretched before him, filled with the prospect of…

Nothing.

The laundry was done, the house was clean, the groceries put away. And Mark was growing tired of the sound of his own voice.

I need company.

He glanced at his phone. *He's probably at work. It's a Monday night. It's only been three days since I saw him.* Except he knew he was going to call. Mark scrolled through his contacts and composed a short text.

Busy?

When there was no immediate reply, he assumed he had his answer. He went into the kitchen and grabbed a beer from the fridge. The moment he popped the cap, his phone rang. He smiled when he saw Dylan's name. "Hey."

"In answer to your question, no, not now. I just finished."

"Do you have any plans for this evening?" *Please say no. Please say no.*

It was then Mark realized just how badly he needed company.

"Yeah, sorry."

Mark suppressed the sigh of disappointment. "Oh. Okay."

"However… if it's a choice between doing something with you, or doing my laundry, you win, hands down."

He chuckled. "Dinner and a movie here?"

"Hmm. That would depend on two factors. What's for dinner, and what's the movie?"

"Dinner is mac and cheese, I'm afraid."

There was a pause. "Homemade mac and cheese, or boxed? Because one of those options leads to my undying adoration and devotion."

Mark laughed. "I'm making it."

"Sorry… Just have to give my phone a quick wipe to get rid of the drool. You said the magic words. I'll sit through a boring-as-whale-shit documentary if it means you feed me homemade mac and cheese."

"I was thinking more along the lines of an action movie. Bangs, car chases, that kind of thing."

"I knew there was a reason why I liked you. When do you want me there?"

Mark felt light as air, and it took him a moment to recognize the emotion. *Fuck me, I'm happy.* "Whenever you can get here."

"That's me you hear ringing your doorbell. You got somewhere safe where I can chain up my bicycle?"

"You're coming by bike?"

"Yeah. I'll get there faster. See you soon." He disconnected.

It was then that it struck him Dylan might also

be in need of company.

Mark walked back into the living room and did a quick survey. It was neat—well, neat-*ish*. He grabbed the laptop, charger, and notebook from the couch, and placed them on the coffee table. The cushions got a pummeling, and his coffee cup was relegated to the kitchen. Then he retrieved the ingredients for dinner.

Five minutes later the doorbell rang. Mark wiped his hands and hurried to open it. Dylan was scanning the exterior of the house, and Mark gestured to the garage. "I'll open it. The bike will be safer in there."

Dylan grinned. "This is Wells. It'll be fine chained to this." He patted the gatepost at the foot of the steps that led up to the front door. Before Mark could get a word out, Dylan had unzipped his jacket, removed a looped chain covered in thick clear plastic, and snaked it around the post and the bike's frame, securing it with a heavy-duty padlock from his pocket. He straightened. "Well? Is dinner made yet?"

Mark laughed out loud. "Get in here, Oh Impatient One. I've just grated the cheese so far."

"I've brought a contribution," Dylan said as he stepped into the house. He snuck his hand inside his jacket once more and removed a bottle of white wine.

"You rode here like that? Thank God you didn't come off the bike. That could've been nasty."

"Well, I couldn't stick it in a pocket, now could I?" Dylan snorted.

"Have you got anything else in there? Dessert? Nibbles?"

Dylan chuckled. "It was uncomfortable enough cycling with a bottle of wine against my ribs." He handed it to Mark. "It'll have to be chilled." A slight frown creased his forehead. "I should've asked if you like wine. I mean, I don't drink it all the time, but it seemed like a nice idea, and I didn't want to turn up empty-hand—"

"Will you just relax? I like wine." Mark peered at the label. "And you did good. This is medium. Perfect."

"Grammy taught me about wine," Dylan confided. "Just the basics. And that was how I got a taste for it. Not that it will ever replace beer in my affections." He patted his chest.

"A man after my own heart." Mark took the bottle into the kitchen and found a space in the fridge for it. "You can sit in here and watch me cook if you like," he called out. A moment later, Dylan stood in the doorway, minus jacket, and Mark gestured to the small table. "Take a seat."

"I like your kitchen," Dylan commented as he pulled out a chair and sat.

"The only thing I don't like about it is this." Mark tapped his foot. "Seventies linoleum. It's gotta go. I'm hoping there are decent floorboards underneath. I'd prefer that." The floor was an intricate pattern in shades of brown.

"So you *are* going to stay here? It's not just a transition house, on your way to someplace else?"

Mark came to a stop. "Want to know something weird? Up until this moment, I hadn't thought about it, but... Yeah, I guess I want to stay." He'd always rented since he'd left home, sharing with other guys, no space, little privacy... Having a space to call his own was...

Bliss.

"What's the rest of the house like?" Dylan

inquired.

Mark arched his eyebrows. "You have a choice. Either I make the dinner, or I give you the guided tour, and *then* I make dinner. Just how hungry are you?"

Dylan laughed. "I'll take the tour. The wine needs time to chill anyway."

"Good point."

Mark took him to the would-be dining room first, and Dylan went over to the pool table, stroking the green felt top. "I'll be honest, I'm not very good. There's a table at the hotel, but I've never had the nerve to pick up a cue and play, in case the manager chooses that moment to walk through."

"He struck me as the sneaky sort."

Dylan snickered. "I swear he's part ninja. We joke that we need to put a bell around his neck, so we know when he's close by." He picked up a cue and gazed longingly at the balls. "Can we play sometime?"

"Sure."

"Are you any good?"

Mark grinned. "Oh yeah. Maybe I can teach you a thing or two." What came to mind were several cheesy scenes he'd done in his twenties, where he'd ended up getting fucked on a pool table, and he quickly shoved them out of his head. He couldn't deny he found Dylan attractive, but that was as far as it went.

Dylan was a friend, and Mark wasn't about to lose that. *And who's to say he'd be interested in being more than that?*

Dylan put down the cue. "Would you mind if we talked about your... work?"

If he were honest, Mark had expected

questions long before this. "Sure." He'd been in the industry too long to be embarrassed by the topic. "What do you want to know?"

Dylan leaned against the table. "Well… You used to work with a couple of studios… but not anymore."

"And you want to know why that is?" Dylan nodded. Mark rolled the eight ball across the table toward him. "The studios got me started, but they called the shots. They decided what I got paid, they chose the content…" He grinned. "And some of the stuff they put out… Christ. Some crazy plots. We're talking pizza delivery boys, stepdads, scenes where I was getting fucked in some guy's bed, and his wife was sleeping right next to him."

"I guess that's what they call suspension of disbelief," Dylan said with a smile.

"And the rest. But once I started working for myself, I got greater control. I choose the content. And the subscribers are great at telling you what they like and don't like. You soon get a feel for what will go down well with them. Three-ways, for example. I always get way more likes when I put out a three-way." When Dylan coughed, Mark chuckled. "I'm guessing you've seen a few of those." He still didn't have Dylan figured out. *Is he just curious, and checking out how the other team bats?*

"Maybe." Dylan cocked his head. "Were there any advantages to working with a studio?"

Mark stroked his beard. "Maybe just one. When it was time to shoot a scene, all I had to do was turn up, flash my latest test results and ID, prep, and off we went. *Everything* was there—sets, equipment… Nowadays, if I want to use something in a shoot, I have to take it with me, or ask if my screen partner has it, to save me the hassle. I've invested in a whole lot of equipment, but sometimes transporting it isn't as easy as you'd think."

"What do you mean?"

Mark crooked his finger. "Step this way." He led Dylan through the house to his bedroom. "I usually store this stuff in the guest bedroom, but I had someone visit recently, so I moved it all."

Dylan's gaze went instantly to the poles standing in the corner, the leather seat propped against them. He walked over to it, his hand outstretched as if to touch it, only to pull it back. "You have a sling."

"Ah, I wondered if you'd seen one." When Dylan rolled his eyes, Mark laughed. "Let me guess. You saw it in one of my videos." He joined Dylan, bending over to pick up one of the long chains. "There was this one studio that had a set fitted out like an honest-to-God dungeon. Chains on the walls and hanging from the ceiling, a St. Andrew's Cross…"

Dylan glanced around the room. "I don't see one of those."

"That's because…" Mark went to his closet door and opened it. "It's in here, in pieces."

Dylan frowned. "Why isn't this stuff assembled?"

"I don't shoot porn here," Mark said simply.

"Okay, but…" Dylan's gaze drifted to the bed, and Mark saw the light.

He ran his hand down one of the bed posts. "I hate to admit it, but the most action this bed has seen is when I toss and turn some nights."

Dylan's face was flushed. "Oh." He gave Mark a quizzical glance. "Do you do that often? Toss and turn, I mean."

"Sometimes." Mark pointed to the chest at the foot of the bed. "Then there's my toy box."

Dylan bit his lip. "Do I wanna know what's in there?"

"You can look. There's nothing gonna leap out at you and bite you." Mark flipped the catch and opened it. Dylan stared at the dildos, vibrators, coils of rope, a couple of floggers, and a host of butt plugs, nipple clamps, and cuffs. He made no move to touch any of the items, however, and Mark wondered if that was out of politeness or a genuine lack of interest.

Maybe he's just vanilla.

"I've got a shoot coming up at the weekend." Mark picked up one of the dildos. "I need to work out what I'm taking with me."

"What kind of scene will it be? If you don't mind me asking," Dylan added quickly.

"A gangbang." Mark quirked an eyebrow.

A deep flush rose up Dylan's neck, staining his cheeks.

Aha.

"At this moment, I have no idea how many guys my buddy is going to squeeze into a small Brooklyn apartment. For all I know, he could be going for a record. I think it's going to be a busy couple of days. The best part is, I'll come home with a ton of footage." *And maybe Joey's right. Maybe this will be my swan song.*

"I think I'm ready to eat now."

Mark got the message—the tour was over.

When they returned to the kitchen, Dylan retook his seat, and Mark couldn't help noticing he sat a little stiffer than previously.

"You okay?" He'd gotten the impression Dylan had wanted to discuss Mark's work, but sometime during the discussion, a switch appeared to have been flipped. The last thing he wanted was to make Dylan uncomfortable.

"Yeah, of course. Why wouldn't I be?"

Why indeed? Mark got on with preparing dinner, and Dylan chatted about movies. It turned out they had similar tastes, but Mark wasn't really listening.

Why does it feel as if I just took a wrong turn?

There *was* one possibility, of course—Dylan was okay with Mark being a porn star in principle, but not so okay when it came to seeing his tools up close.

It's not as if I haven't encountered that reaction before. Maybe Dylan wasn't so different after all. Then he realized there was another possibility—information overload. *Maybe he got more than he bargained for.*

By the time they sat down to eat, Dylan's awkward mood seemed to have evaporated, and Mark was profoundly grateful. Having Dylan feel comfortable around him was important. Not for the first time that evening, one thought consumed him.

I don't want to lose this.

Except there was more to Dylan than mere friendship. There was a mystery to be solved, and Mark was a sucker for a good mystery. It was obvious something about their discussion had embarrassed Dylan, but why? He'd told Mark he had four gay friends. They seemed to be the same age as him, which meant one thing in Mark's mind—they would talk about sex. Most gay guys of Mark's acquaintance did that a lot.

Then what's the problem?

Dylan closed his bedroom door, bolted it, and flopped onto the bed.

Christ.

The food had been great, the movie fantastic, and the company perfect. And yet… All through the evening, Dylan had kept sneaking glances at Mark beside him on the couch, only to look away when Mark turned his head toward him.

What am I doing?

It didn't help that Dylan knew what lay hidden beneath Mark's clothing. A glance at Mark's crotch had sent heat rushing through him as he pictured the long, heavy dick he'd watched so often.

The same dick he'd imagined slowly penetrating him, taking his breath away.

But what stuck in Dylan's mind most was Mark's bedroom. *Talk about a treasure trove.* He could have spent *hours* sifting through the contents of that toy box. Keeping his hands to himself had taken a real effort, and all because he didn't want Mark to see how badly he ached to touch, stroke, discover…

Regret consumed him. *I shouldn't have held back.*

What soured his evening had been the knowledge that Mark was preparing to shoot more scenes. Dylan knew it was his living, but still… He also knew what lay at the root of his unhappiness.

I don't want to imagine how it would feel anymore. I

want to know.

Chapter Twelve

September 27

Mark took a moment to stretch his back. He'd been working on his laptop for the past hour, trying to edit the hours of footage into something more focused and sleeker. Doing a lot of POV recording meant he'd have enough for two very different videos, possibly three. He had to admit, Joey had pulled out all the stops. They'd ended up with eight guys on and around the bed, and Mark still had no clue how they'd managed it.

His gaze drifted to his phone. There'd been a text from Dylan shortly after Mark had arrived home. After several days of radio silence, he'd been relieved, even though it was only a couple of lines.

I missed him. Hopefully, they could fit in a sightseeing trip during the week. Mark needed to recharge his batteries and do some serious thinking about his future.

He also wanted to spend some time with Dylan.

Do I share what's in my thoughts? Maybe Dylan would have some ideas. It wasn't as if he knew nothing about Mark's present state of mind, so the idea of him seeking pastures new wouldn't come as a total surprise. *And two heads are better than one, don't they say?*

The doorbell made him jump, and Mark glanced at the wall clock. *Who's here this late on Sunday night?* He went to the window and peered through.

Dylan stood there, chaining up his bicycle.

What the hell?

Mark opened the front door. "Hey. Did I miss a text or something?" Dylan had said nothing about coming over.

"Can I come in? I know it's late, but I finished about ten minutes ago, and…"

"Sure." Mark stood aside to let him enter. He smiled as he shut the door. "Actually, I was thinking about you seconds before you rang the bell." He waited until Dylan had removed his jacket and hung it on a hook. "You want some coffee, tea…?"

"Got anything stronger?"

Okay, now Mark was concerned. "There's beer."

Dylan nodded. "That would be good."

Mark left him in the living room and headed for the kitchen. "When I didn't hear from you, I wondered if I'd done something," he called out.

"I had a lot to think about, and I couldn't talk to you until I was ready."

Mark blinked. That sounded ominous. "When's your day off this week?"

"Tomorrow."

And whatever this is couldn't wait until then? Mark grabbed the two opened bottles and went back to the living room. "You have my complete attention. What's up?"

Dylan was sitting on the couch, leaning forward, his gaze locked on the laptop screen where Mark had frozen a frame: Joey was riding Mark's cock, while Chaz sucked Joey's dick. Another guy stood on the bed, and Mark was swallowing his dick to the root. Three guys stood around the bed, priming their boners.

"I'll get rid of that," Mark said hurriedly. He put the bottles down and went to grab the laptop.

Dylan stopped him, blocking Mark's hand with his arm. He pointed to the screen. "That. *That's* the problem."

Mark's stomach clenched. *Aw fuck*. He'd really hoped Dylan would be different. "I get it. Well, I think I do."

Dylan frowned. "What is it you think you get?"

"I've had boyfriends who couldn't cope with this, but I didn't expect the same reaction from a friend."

Dylan sighed. "No, you don't get it at *all*."

Mark sat beside him. "Then you tell me what's going on."

Dylan stared at the screen. "I've lost count of how many times I've watched you. I see the way you look at these guys. God, the moans when you're fucking them… You're so… into them. And every time I watched, I thought… what I wouldn't give to have… someone look at me like that. Because I've never had anyone do that."

"But what you see on the screen isn't real," Mark protested. "Those looks? The sounds? It's all for the camera. And what ends up on your phone or laptop or tablet is nothing like what actually took place. It's an end product." Then he had an idea. "Watch this." He hit the Play button.

"I've seen your stuff, remember?" Dylan remonstrated.

"Not like this you haven't." Mark sat back, and on the screen, the action stopped, followed by a discussion of positions. Chaz told Joey not to go so deep, and Mark admonished—*what was his name? Leroy?*—for the same thing. Then more lube was applied, before whoever was filming at the time yelled at them to get their act together. What followed was a stop-start-stop-start process that Mark knew went on for a while, as they tried different configurations. There was laughter, a lot of laughter, and it had been fun at times, but it bore little resemblance to what would be the finished article.

He hit pause. "You see? *That's* the reality."

Dylan's face fell. "No, no, no. Don't show me this. That isn't what I want."

"What do you mean?"

He turned to face Mark, his expression miserable. "I want the lie. I want that… intimacy I see in every one of your videos." His breathing hitched. "I… I want you to look at *me* the way you look at… at…" He pulled his phone from his pocket, tapped the screen, and then held it up. "At him."

It was a screenshot of one of Mark's scenes. Mark was fucking a guy missionary, looking into his eyes, the guy's legs resting on Mark's shoulders, and the camera angle focused on Mark's face. In a heartbeat, Mark realized two things: he understood completely what Dylan meant about intimacy, and he was confused as fuck.

He raised his head and gazed at Dylan. "What do you want?"

Dylan appeared so fucking torn. "I… I want you to touch me. To look at me as if I *matter*. My whole fucking life, none of my feelings, my thoughts, my opinions… none of them mattered to my family."

Mark was lost for words. Because Dylan *couldn't* be asking for… He wasn't asking Mark to…

Was he?

Dylan took in the space between them, the way Mark held himself so still… And then he saw the light. "I get it. You don't want me like that." He got up from the couch, his limbs so freaking heavy. "I'm sorry I disturbed you, especially when you're so… busy." He froze. "Jesus. I sound just like my parents. They have passive-aggressive down to an art. I'm sorry. I shouldn't have said that. I guess some things kinda seep in whether you want them to or not." He walked toward the front door.

"Wait! Stop." Feet thumped across the floor, and suddenly Mark was blocking his path. He gripped Dylan's shoulders, forcing him to halt. "Before I do anything that could be misconstrued, I want you to admit something."

Dylan's heart hammered. "Admit what?"

"Anything!" Mark retorted. "Whatever it is you're trying so hard not to tell me. Because I'm not making a move until you do."

Dylan stared at him. "I… I can't."

"Yes, you can," Mark said in a gentle voice. "You've come this far. Just a little further. Let it out, because I promise you, it'll be so much better when you do."

Lord, how he yearned to believe that.

Then his chest loosened, and his breathing became that little bit easier. *Tell him.*

Dylan sucked in a deep breath. "I think I'm… bi. Well, I'm pretty sure I am."

Mark's smile sent warmth racing through him. "*That's* what I was waiting for." His eyes sparkled. "I was right, wasn't I? Doesn't it feel good to let it out?"

Good? Dylan could get drunk on the euphoria coursing through him. Then he stilled as Mark took his hand. It wasn't the touching he'd had in mind, but he'd take it.

"Dylan… what do you want from me? Be honest." Dylan gazed at him in confusion, and Mark's smile faded, replaced by an intense gaze. "You're driving the bus now. Where are we going from here?"

Fuck, where could he start?

"Touch me?"

Mark took a step toward him, bringing Dylan's hand to his chest, and Dylan's heartbeat quickened. "Because you were honest with me, I'll show you the same courtesy." Closer still, until their bodies were almost touching. "You were wrong, you know." Mark lowered his voice as he leaned in. "About me not wanting you like that." His fingers were gentle under Dylan's chin. "I care for you, for our friendship. That means a lot to me. But…" He looked Dylan in the eye, and Dylan's heart danced. "I think you're a gorgeous, sexy man. I've thought that from the moment we met. And ever since then, I've wanted to do… this."

Warm lips met his, and Dylan couldn't help

himself. He opened for Mark, breathing him in, drawing the scent of him into his nostrils, his heart soaring at the first touch of Mark's tongue against his. It was the kiss he'd craved for so long, and he didn't want it to end.

Then Mark pulled away, and Dylan took a moment to regain control. He gave Mark a hard stare. "You stopped."

Mark smiled. "You're observant."

"But I don't want you to stop."

Mark took a step back, and Dylan had to fight the urge to wrap his arms around him. "I'll need something from you before we venture any further."

"Permission to continue? You've got it."

Mark grinned. "Ah, but permission to do what, exactly?" Then he sighed. "It's late, I'm exhausted, your head is about to come off... so I'm sending you on your way—with a little homework."

Pain speared Dylan's chest, and something roiled deep in his gut. "You... you do still want me, don't you?"

Mark widened his eyes. "Yes. God, yes." He cupped Dylan's face between his hands and held him still as he zeroed in on Dylan's mouth, claiming his lips in a firm, chaste kiss. When he broke it, his forehead met Dylan's, and he let out another soft sigh. "There's so much I want to do with you, but I need you to do something for me first."

"What?"

Mark's fingers were gentle on his face. "You've watched enough porn to have an idea of what you want to experience... right?" Dylan nodded, his cheeks burning. "Then what I want you to do is write them down in two lists."

Dylan reared back. "You weren't kidding about homework." Mark's words sank in. "*Two* lists?"

Mark nodded, "The first is all those things you don't mind me seeing. The second? That one is just for you. Call it a wish list, all the things you want to do, but don't have the nerve to ask for. Maybe one day I'll get to see it, maybe never."

"But… why write them down if you never get to see them?"

"That list isn't for me—it's for you. A kind of… therapy." Mark's steady gaze sent a ripple of heat through him. "Maybe there are things you want that you think I'd judge you for, activities you're ashamed to want. Writing them down? It's just a way of being honest with yourself. The time to hide is over. Like I said, you don't have to let me see those. But list one, I definitely get to read that." He leaned in, and this time the kiss was less chaste, more heated. "All those things you've seen on your phone, or laptop… The things that make you hot under the collar, make you hard…"

"And then?" Just *thinking* about some of the activities he knew would be on his list had Dylan's shaft solid as a rock.

"Then… you share them with me, and we take it one step at a time."

"That sounds kind of… slow."

Mark's eyes twinkled. "Nothing wrong with slow." He curved his hand around Dylan's cheek. "I don't have many friends, and the ones I do have, I want to hold onto." His hand was on Dylan's nape, holding him there. "I won't do anything that jeopardizes this relationship."

"Do we have one of those?"

"There are many definitions of relationship."

Firm fingers stroked the back of Dylan's head. "Yes, it can mean a sexual involvement, but it also means a connection, emotional or otherwise. We already have a connection—we just want to… change it up a little. Develop it."

"When we first met? Okay, lust *might* have been the overriding emotion, I'll admit that. But then I got to know you." Dylan shuddered out a breath. "I don't want to lose you either."

Mark kissed his forehead. "I'm glad." He put space between them. "Tomorrow. Let's meet at the Cove Café for breakfast. We are *not* going to discuss your list, okay? Not in public. Then as it's your day off, we can come back here and… take it from there."

Even though Mark was saying all the right things, Dylan couldn't escape the fear and panic that trickled through him. *He's still sending me away.*

Mark closed the gap between them, and two strong arms encircled him. Mark's breath fluttered against his ear. "You need to hold onto one thing while we're apart. As much as you want me? I want you too." He slid his hands lower, and Dylan caught his breath as Mark molded Dylan's body to his.

There was no mistaking that hardness.

Mark focused his eyes on Dylan's. "You see?" He kissed Dylan's neck before whispering, "That's for you."

"Jesus, my heart."

Mark chuckled. "*Your* heart? You should feel what mine's doing."

"Thank you," Dylan said quietly.

"There's nothing to thank me for."

"Yet."

Mark stilled. "About what you said. You

matter to *me*, you got that? You matter very much."

It was the best thing he could have said.

Mark bit his lip. "Now, are you safe to be let loose on that bicycle, or should I drive you home?"

Dylan laughed. "I haven't lost my sense of balance." His head was spinning, however, and a million butterflies fluttered in his stomach.

Mark walked him to the door, grabbed his jacket, and held it while Dylan slipped his arms into the sleeves. "Try to sleep?"

Dylan snorted. "You're kidding, right? I'm going to be doing my homework."

Mark let out a wry chuckle as he opened the door. "I have a feeling this is going to be interesting."

Dylan had a feeling there was no way he was going to share list two.

As he waved goodbye and began the trip home, Dylan's mind was racing, the same thoughts tumbling through his brain over and over.

He wants me.

He said yes.

Chapter Thirteen

September 28

Mark sipped his coffee, his gaze trained on the window, watching for Dylan. He'd arrived early at the café, his stomach grumbling. Mark wasn't sure if that was due to hunger or anticipation. He felt as if his whole body was vibrating, leaving him energized, his pulse rapid.

When was I ever this excited?

Then he remembered. He'd caused a stir at the studio the day he auditioned. They'd asked him about his experience with guys, and he'd confessed to being a virgin. Judging by the looks and snickers he'd received, Mark had guessed they heard that a lot. When he explained he'd never had sex before, the guys in the room had grinned. His audition scene had been short—Mark figured it had taken him less than ten minutes to coax his dick to total hardness, and less than three minutes after that to shoot his load. The guy behind the camera had seemed pleased, however, and the studio head had offered him a contract as soon as he'd cleaned up.

My first time... It had only been a blow job scene, but he'd thought his heart would explode, he was so keyed up. They'd paired him up with the hottest guy Mark had ever seen, and thankfully, Brian had taken his time, showing an unexpected gentleness that had eased Mark's quaking heart.

Mark intended being as gentle with Dylan.

"Earth to Mark, come in, Mark."

He jumped. Dylan stood next to his table, grinning. Mark gave him a mock glare. "Have you been taking ninja lessons from that manager of yours?"

Dylan pulled out the chair facing him and sat. "Sorry. You were zoned out. Have you been waiting long?"

"Not really. I haven't ordered yet. I was waiting for you." Dylan reached for the menu and winced. Mark frowned. "What's up?"

"It's nothing. I'm just a little stiff this morning." He rolled his eyes when Mark chuckled. "Will you stop that? I fell asleep sitting up in bed last night, and when I woke, I ached like a son of a bitch."

"I thought I told you to get some sleep?"

"I did—I was just in the wrong position, that's all. And it's your fault."

Mark gaped. "How is it my fault?"

"Because I stayed up way too late doing… research for *your* lists." Dylan rubbed his shoulder.

Mark smiled. "I was going to ask if you'd done your homework. Without getting into specifics, of course." He inclined his head toward the nearest table, where two sweet-looking old ladies were chatting animatedly over their coffee and French toast.

Dylan glanced in their direction, and coughed. "Yeah, let's not do that."

"What do you want for breakfast?" Mark asked. "I'm going for that omelet I had last time."

"Yeah, that sounds good." Dylan picked up the coffee pot. "This'll help."

Mark laughed and got up to walk to the counter. He gave their order, and when he returned to the table, Dylan was clearly trying to get comfortable. Mark assessed him for a moment before speaking. "You know what you need?"

"A good night's sleep in a horizontal position?" Dylan quipped.

"A massage. I can give you a rubdown when we get to my house." Dylan blinked, and Mark had to laugh again. "Okay, I didn't mean for that to come out as sleazy as it did. I really do give a great massage." He smiled and leaned in. "And you did say 'touch me', didn't you?" He straightened in his chair.

That got him a laugh. "Yeah, I did. And yes, I did my homework, sir."

"I must admit, I'm intrigued to see the size of your… list."

Dylan smothered a snort.

He tilted his head to one side. "Do you feel better today? Apart from the aches, I mean."

Dylan nodded. "I'm buzzing though."

Mark leaned forward again. "Me too," he confided in a whisper.

Dylan's eyes went wide. "But why? I mean… this is what you do, isn't it?"

"Sure, but this is the start of an adventure. I get to explore… with you."

"And I get to discover." For a moment, Dylan's eyes had a faraway look. Then he smiled. "Something someone said to me this summer. I'm finally acting on his advice."

Mark helped himself to more coffee. "Can I ask you something? How long have you been thinking about this?"

Dylan bit his lip. "Let's just say a while."

Mark had to ask the question that had niggled him for days. "Did you think about confiding in your friends?" The bob of Dylan's Adam's apple had him backpedaling. "Forget I asked. It's none of my business."

"No, you're right. I could've talked about this with them, but…"

Mark studied him for a moment, taking in the obvious swallow, the glance away, the too quick smile… *There's something you're not telling me, isn't there?* He wasn't going to push. *Maybe whatever it is that's eating away at you is on your second list.*

Dylan might never reveal its contents, and Mark could live with that.

Their breakfasts arrived, and for ten minutes or so, neither of them spoke. It wasn't an uncomfortable silence, for which Mark was grateful. He wanted Dylan at his ease.

A good massage would help with that. As for what came after, Mark was playing that by ear.

"You were right, you know." Dylan's voice was quiet.

"About what?"

Dylan wiped his lips with his napkin. "It did feel so much better when I finally got the words out."

Mark's instincts told him there were more revelations to come. "Still buzzing?"

"God, yes." Dylan leaned closer. "I'm excited, but…"

"You're nervous too. I know. I may be in my thirties, but I can remember all the emotions colliding inside me. My job is to make the experience good for you." He grinned. "No pressure then."

Dylan shuddered out a breath. "I trust you."

Mark smiled. "Thank you." He gestured to their empty plates. "Now, do you want to stay here chatting, or do you want to go someplace where I can kiss you again?"

Judging by Dylan's slow exhalation, he knew which option they were going for.

By the time they reached Mark's house, Dylan's heart was pounding, his body tingled, and *everywhere* felt warm. Mark had no sooner shut the front door than Dylan thrust a folded sheet of paper into his hand. "Here." It had been burning a hole in his pocket all the way through breakfast. Then he removed his boots.

Mark bit back a smile. "No kiss?" He took the list and pocketed it, then drew Dylan into his arms. "I've been wanting to do this ever since you walked into the café."

Dylan relished the feel of Mark's lips on his, Mark's hands on his back, his nape, Mark's firm chest pressed to his own. It was no quick peck, but a lingering, deliberate Well-hello-there kiss, and Dylan's nerves ebbed away with each passing moment.

"That's better," Mark murmured against his neck, the words vibrating through him, creating an almost ticklish sensation. "Now, let's look at this list."

He led Dylan to the couch, and they sat. Mark reached into his pocket, and just like that, Dylan's heartbeat picked up a little speed. Mark unfolded the sheet and studied it. "Okay, not as long as I thought it would be."

It was shorter than Dylan would have liked, but that was only because some of his ideas had been assigned to the second list. After a lot of research—*okay, watching porn*—he'd come up with his absolute definites:

> *Handjob*
> *BJ - receive and give*
> *69*
> *Rimming - receive and give*
> *Fingers*
> *Fuck*

Mark met his gaze. "This is everything?"

No, it isn't, but it's everything I felt able to share at this point. "Yes."

"Okay. Fingers… in your ass, I presume." Mark studied the list again. "Can I put anything else in there? Maybe some toys?"

Christ. Dylan's throat seized. "I… I could be up for that." The words came out as a croak, making him sound like a strangled frog.

Mark's eyes were warm. "Breathe, Dylan. This is a good list, but I'm just clarifying some details." He gave him an inquiring glance. "Have you ever done anal?

Dylan tried to drag air into his lungs. "I suggested it to a girl once. You'd think I'd asked her to roll in dog shit, she was that disgusted."

Mark regarded him with obvious interest. "Since you brought the subject up… how much experience do you have?"

"A little," Dylan admitted. "I'm not a virgin, if that's what you're asking."

Mark's smile grew wicked. "Your hole is."

Holy fuck.

Mark's hand was on his thigh, stroking, touching... "That makes you hot, doesn't it? Are you thinking about me sliding a finger in there?"

Fuck.

He leaned in, his breath warm on Dylan's ear. "What about my cock?"

Dylan sprang back. "Okay, okay, I think you just proved you can turn me on in a heartbeat." Christ, his dick was throbbing.

Mark cupped his cheek. "You set the pace, remember? Like I said last night, you're driving the bus." He removed his hand, and Dylan ached to have it return. "But how about we start with that massage?"

He took a deep breath. "Sounds great."

Mark's hand covered his. "Just remember. Anytime you want a breather, or it gets too overwhelming, you tell me, okay? A simple *Stop* will suffice." Then he stood, took Dylan's hand, and led him through the house to his bedroom. "I don't have one of those fancy massage tables, so the bed will have to do. Let me grab some oils and towels, while you get undressed." He turned to face Dylan, his eyes sparkling. "Unless you'd like me to do that?"

Jesus, there went his heart again.

"I think I can manage." Dylan waited until Mark had left the room before removing his jacket and sweater. He did his best to avoid looking at the bed, because every time he saw the white sheets and the lube on the nightstand his shivers multiplied. His fingers trembled as he popped the button on his jeans. "How much am I taking off?" he called out.

"All of it."

Dylan pushed his jeans past his hips, taking his briefs with them. He stepped out of his clothing and folded everything neatly, laying them over the footboard.

"I like a man who's neat." Mark walked to the side of the bed, deposited a bottle of oil on the nightstand, and opened up a large white towel. He glanced at Dylan, and Dylan's dick jerked. Mark smiled. "Thank you."

"For what?"

"I'm the first guy who gets to see you naked. And before you say a word, the locker room at high school doesn't count." He looked Dylan up and down. "I'll be honest. I've spent a bit of time imagining you without your clothes." His eyes sparkled. "I'm not disappointed in the least." He gestured to the towel. "Lie down, please. On your front." His lips twitched. "Which might be a little uncomfortable, given your present state."

Despite his nerves, Dylan chuckled. "I blame you." He climbed onto the bed and stretched out along its center. Mark removed his tee, and Dylan's pulse quickened at the sight of the ripped body he could have described blindfolded.

"Just to put us on an equal footing…" Mark unfastened his jeans and shoved them to his ankles. He bent to remove them, and Dylan caught a glimpse of Mark's ass.

"When did you have that done?" He pointed to Mark's ass cheek, where the words *Fuck Me* were tattooed. He'd seen it God knew how many times, of course.

"Years ago. Everyone was getting tattoos, but I didn't want a sleeve, or anything elaborate, so I decided to keep it simple—and direct."

Dylan managed a chuckle. "Yeah, nothing ambiguous about that." Then Mark turned, and Dylan's line of sight was perfect for a close-up of Mark's dick. "Wow." It was thicker than it appeared on the screen, and his hole tightened involuntarily.

"Nothing you haven't already seen, right?" Mark teased.

"Seeing you on the screen is one thing, but in real life…" Dylan grinned. "To quote you, I'm not disappointed in the least."

Mark pointed to the pillows. "Head down, please."

Dylan tore his gaze away and laid his head on the pillow. He jumped when oil trickled onto his back.

"Sorry. I should have warmed it first." Mark put the bottle down and got onto the bed beside him. "You ever had a massage before?"

"No, never."

"I usually ask if the person being massaged wants me to go hard or soft, or deep."

Dylan chuckled. "I'm going to trust you know what you're doing." Then Mark's hands were on his neck and shoulders, and damn, it felt amazing. "Oh, that's nice."

"I haven't even gotten started yet." Mark shifted his hands lower, using his thumbs to push into the flesh, and Dylan groaned.

"Right there."

"Gotcha." Then the pressure changed.

"What… what are you doing that with?"

"My elbow. I'm applying it to various pressure points. Is it okay?"

It was way better than merely okay. "It feels really good. Where did you learn to do this?" Mark moved lower still, and Dylan moaned as he kneaded the top of his thighs, digging deep into the muscle.

"A guy I roomed with in Vegas. He was a trained masseur, and he taught me a few things."

"Either he was a really good teacher, or you're a natural at this." Dylan turned his head to the side. "You wanted a career change? You could do this." He tried not to stare at Mark's dick that jutted toward him, bobbing as Mark moved.

Mark chuckled. "Giving massages to friends is one thing—doing it for a living requires proper training, specialist knowledge."

"What's to stop you getting it? I'm being serious." Then he groaned as Mark kneaded his lower back, just above his ass. "Fuck, right there."

"That's a result of your sleeping position last night. Now close your eyes, and let me loosen you up."

Dylan did as instructed, and it wasn't long before Mark's gentle hands lulled him into a doze, massaging the length of his body, all the way to his feet. It wasn't sexual, more sensual, and Dylan lost himself in Mark's firm strokes and manipulations.

Mark returned to his shoulders. "Does that feel better?"

"So much, you wouldn't believe."

"Good. Because I'm going to change things up a little."

Then his breathing hitched as Mark caressed his ass cheeks, his warm, slick hands sliding through

Dylan's crack. "I love your ass."

"I love the way you touch my ass." He groaned as Mark dug his fingers into the flesh, kneading upward with a firm stroke.

Mark chuckled, and Dylan smothered a gasp as Mark rubbed over his pucker before changing position to work on his inner thighs, his fingers skating perilously close to Dylan's balls. There was a momentary pause, and then oil trickled over his ass. With one hand resting on Dylan's lower back, Mark reached between Dylan's legs and freed his cock, working it with slick fingers.

"This okay?"

Dylan tilted his ass and spread his legs a little, wanting more of Mark's touch, and Mark teased the head of his dick with his fingertips. "I'll take that as a yes." Then he rubbed his thumb over Dylan's pucker, and Dylan squirmed, unable to stay still a moment longer. He humped the bed as Mark stroked firm fingers over his hole, his balls, right to the head of his cock.

"Maybe you should flip over," Mark suggested.

Dylan's heartbeat shifted into a higher gear, and he rolled over, his stiffening dick against his belly. Mark's eyes gleamed. "That brings me nicely to the first item on your list, although I have a feeling we might be crossing off more than one this morning." Before Dylan could ask which ones, Mark wrapped his hand around Dylan's shaft. Then with his right hand, he grabbed Dylan's and brought it to his own rigid cock.

Oh God. Mark's dick was warm and silky to the touch, and it fitted perfectly into the funnel of Dylan's hand.

"You said hand job, but you weren't specific." Mark grinned. "So I thought I'd use my initiative." He gave Dylan's cock a slow pull. "Show me how you like it. Work my dick like it was your own."

"Can I... can I kneel up?"

Mark let go of his shaft and hauled him upright, until they were both kneeling, facing each other. "That better?" Then his hand was back, tugging on Dylan's dick, matching Dylan's strokes on Mark's cock. "That's it. Just like that."

They found their rhythm, working in harmony, and Dylan loved every second of it. Mark shifted closer, sandwiching his heavy dick between them, rolling his hips to slide it up and down Dylan's belly, leaving a sticky trail of pre-cum with each glide.

It was hot as fuck, and when Mark leaned in to kiss him, it was perfect. One hand on Dylan's nape, the other on his ass, he undulated his body against Dylan's, their lips locked. Dylan was on *fire*.

"I don't think I can last much longer," he confessed.

Mark shifted quickly to kneel behind him, and Dylan caught the *click* of the lube bottle. Then a slick cock insinuated itself between his ass cheeks, and Mark reached around him with an equally slick hand to grasp Dylan's shaft. Mark rocked his hips, sliding his dick over Dylan's hole as he worked Dylan's cock, gathering pace. When Mark tweaked Dylan's nipple with his fingers, it was all over, and Dylan groaned as he shot onto the bed, pulse after pulse of cum until he was trembling in Mark's arms.

"Fuck, you're beautiful when you come," Mark groaned. He held Dylan upright, kissing his neck and shoulders.

"But you haven't," Dylan remonstrated.

"Then you'd better see to that." Mark flopped onto his back, his dick hard and thick. "Kiss me while you jerk me off."

Dylan lay beside him, and Mark stroked his nape as they kissed. He curled his fingers around Mark's dick and slid his hand up and down the heavy shaft, Mark pushing his hips off the bed as he drove his cock faster through the slick tunnel. He moaned into the kiss, and the sound sent Dylan's spirits soaring.

Warmth creamed his hand, and Dylan exulted in the knowledge that *he'd* done that, he'd brought Mark to the edge. He deepened their kiss, his breathing rapid, aware of each jolt of Mark's body against his. On impulse, he broke the kiss and leaned over to flick Mark's nipple with his tongue, loving the shudders that coursed through him.

At last, Mark was still, his cock limp in Dylan's hand. Dylan looked into his eyes. "Was that okay?"

Mark grinned. "I was about to ask you the same question."

Dylan let go of Mark's dick and rolled onto his back. Mark lay on his side, rubbing Dylan's belly and chest with a leisurely motion. "I think I was more nervous than you."

Dylan stared at him. "Why would you be nervous?"

"Because you've wanted this for a long time, haven't you? I didn't want to disappoint you."

"Disappoint—come here." Dylan tugged Mark to lie on top of him, and enfolded him in his arms. "That was the most amazing thing I've ever experienced." Mark's weight on him, pinning him to the mattress, sent the most delicious thoughts flitting through his head.

Mark's eyes were bright. "But we've barely started."

Dylan chuckled. "Then what are we waiting for? What's next?"

Mark kissed him, a slow, sensual kiss that sent warmth hurtling through him. "Hey, I thought we were taking things slow." He scraped his fingers through Dylan's hair. "So how does it feel, being naked with a guy?"

Dylan did a swift assessment. "It should feel weird, but… it feels right."

Except *right* didn't get anywhere *near* how it felt.

"That's because you're not hiding anymore." Mark's gaze intensified. "Well, not quite. You still have your secrets."

A trickle of unease filtered through him. "Doesn't everyone?"

Mark sat up, shifting across the bed. "I know what I said, but I've changed my mind. I want to know what it is you're not telling me."

He stiffened. "I don't know what you mean."

Mark gave a soft sigh. "I thought I was okay not knowing, but… twice now when I've asked a certain question, I've clearly touched a nerve, and each time I backed off. Well, I got to thinking that maybe whatever you're hiding is important. And it has to be something huge, if you've hidden it from your closest friends." He looked Dylan in the eye. "You told me how good it felt when you finally came out and said you were bi."

Dylan nodded, his throat tight.

"I'm willing to bet you'll feel an even bigger release when you share what's eating away at you."

Dylan tried to swallow, but his mouth was dry. "How... how did you know?"

"Remember I said I don't have many friends? Well, with the ones I do have?" Mark smiled. "I pay attention." He cupped Dylan's chin. "I'm right, aren't I?"

Dylan managed another nod.

"What scares you? The thought that whatever it is will make me see you in a different light?"

"Yes," Dylan whispered.

Mark kissed him, a light, sweet kiss. "There is nothing you can say that is going to scare me off, okay? Because I've seen a lot these past seventeen years. So please, stop worrying about it, and just tell me, so we can move past this."

Tell him. Because Mark was right. It *was* eating away at him. But the shame that had plagued him for so long clung on stubbornly. "What if I don't tell you... but I show you?"

"Show me what?"

"My second list."

Chapter Fourteen

Mark's heart hammered. *Breakthrough*. He couldn't shake the idea that this list lay at the root of Dylan's anxiety. "Get it for me."

Dylan crawled to the foot of the bed, and Mark had to fight hard not to be distracted by that gorgeous ass. *This is not the time*. Dylan grabbed his jacket, and reached into his inside pocket. He removed the folded paper, staring at it.

Mark held out his hand for it. "You've gotten this far, don't stop now." He gave Dylan a hopefully warm smile. "I'm not about to judge you, okay? I might even be able to help. Because I'm assuming that whatever you want to tell me will be made really obvious once I read that list." He patted the empty space next to him. "Come sit here."

Dylan crawled up the bed and sat beside him, placing the folded paper into his hand. Mark unfolded the sheet and scanned it. *Oh Dylan*. He smiled. It was shorter than the previous list, but infinitely more revealing.

Bondage
St. Andrew's Cross
Spanking
Sling

Mark put the paper on the nightstand, aware of Dylan's posture, his averted gaze, the way he seemed almost to… crumple before Mark's eyes.

"It's okay," he said in a low voice. Dylan's gaze met his, and Mark knew he needed something more affirming than that. He cupped Dylan's chin and turned his face gently toward Mark's. "So you're a bit… kinky. Not a damn thing wrong with that."

It was as if his words opened up the floodgates.

Dylan shuddered, leaning into him. "I thought there was something wrong with me for wanting this."

"Why would you think that?"

He shivered. "There's this girl at the hotel, Della… We dated, a long time ago, when I first started working there. And one night, I asked her if we could try something a little different."

Mark was intrigued. "What was your suggestion?"

"I… I wanted her to tie me to the bed and then ride me."

"And? What's wrong with that?"

Dylan blinked and straightened. "See, *you* sit there and ask that as if getting tied up during sex is totally natural, but Della was horrified."

Aw fuck. "So it was just bad luck that the first girl you were brave enough to be honest with, was vanilla from head to toe." Mark tilted his head to one side. "I'm guessing you thought you were some kind of deviant."

"She made me feel as if I was," Dylan protested. "And she said as much. For weeks, months after, I was scared shitless she was going to tell everyone I worked with. So scared that I avoided asking anyone out on a date."

"Oh sweetheart." The endearment was out

before he had time to rein it in. He pulled Dylan into his arms. "There is absolutely nothing wrong with you, okay?" He kissed his temple. "Why didn't you talk about this with your gay friends?"

"Because none of them are into that kinda stuff!"

"How do you know?"

Dylan sighed. "They've never mentioned anything like… that."

Mark tried not to smile. "Just because they don't talk about it doesn't mean they're not doing it. Maybe they like to keep that side of things private. I'd be willing to bet your friends get up to some real kinky shit behind closed doors."

"You think?"

Mark nodded. "And here's the bit you'll like. They do *not* need to know that you're into all this. Because what you do in the privacy of your own bedroom is no one's business but yours."

Dylan stared at him in silence, then sagged against him. "You were right again. We needed to talk about this. The thing is, I'd built it up in my mind, until just the *thought* of telling another living soul filled me with dread."

Mark had an idea. "Would you feel more comfortable discussing this over a cup of tea or coffee?"

Dylan's eyes lit up. "Can we?"

Mark laughed. "Of course. Do you want to get dressed, or put on one of my robes?"

Dylan hesitated for a moment. "Robe, please."

That revealed a lot. "Fine. Let me grab a couple, and then we can go sit on the couch and talk." Dylan's slow exhale told him he'd said the right thing.

"Thank you." Dylan kissed him, his hand on Mark's neck, and the sweetness of it was a reminder.

Take it slow. Mark wasn't going to take another step until Dylan was ready for it.

Dylan nestled against the seat cushions, a cup of fragrant tea in his hands. "This is… surreal."

"What's surreal about tea?" Mark asked.

"Well, nothing, it's just the fact that we're naked under these robes. And it's daylight out there."

Oh my God, he's so fucking adorable.

Mark grinned. "That's what makes it fun. Sexy." He cleared his throat. "So… let's talk about your second list."

"What's to talk about? You've seen it now."

"Sure I have, and it's a little vague. But there's another far more important conversation we need to have."

"Oh?" Dylan's frown disappeared. "Oh. You mean safe sex."

"Exactly."

Dylan gave him a thoughtful glance. "You don't use condoms on your videos."

"That's true, most of the time, but only when I know my partner's status. Most of the guys I shoot with are on PrEP. Do you know what that is?" He wasn't about to make assumptions.

"I've read about it. Doesn't it prevent HIV?"

Mark nodded. "What it *doesn't* do is protect against STIs. So… I get tested regularly. Some guys get tested every three months, some every six. Because sex is an important part of what I do, I go to a clinic once a month. And whoever I film with has to show me their latest results. No results, no shoot."

"Does that mean we don't need… anything?"

Mark smiled. "I have a new box of condoms in my closet. We *will* be using them." Dylan grimaced, but Mark wasn't going to be swayed on this. "I'm not fond of them either, but it's better to be safe."

"And if I get tested too?"

"Then we'll talk again." Mark tapped the list beside him on the arm of the couch. "Now… spanking. I know *so* many guys who liked to be spanked, some of them during sex, so you are definitely not alone in that one. Bondage… you mentioned being tied to the bed. Is that what you want?"

"I… I like the idea of being… helpless, not able to move, unable to… stop you."

Mark grinned. "I like that idea too. Maybe once you've gotten used to having a dick in your ass. Which leads me to my next point. Do you want that? Or do you just want to top?"

Dylan flushed. "Can I do both?"

He laughed. "Hell yeah." He peered at the list. "About the sling…"

"I saw one of your videos where you fucked a guy in a sling. You just… pounded his ass."

"And you want to be pounded, is that it?" When Dylan's flush deepened, Mark reached over and stroked his bare thigh where the robe had slipped. "I refer you to my previous remark. I'm not going to slam into you the first time, okay? If anything, I'll be gentle." Dylan expelled a breath, and Mark squeezed his leg. "If you're going to enjoy this, then you need to communicate. Don't hold anything back, all right?" He tapped the remaining item on the list. "The St. Andrew's Cross…"

"I just want to try it. I mean, I don't want you to flog me, or anything like that, just… tie me to it?" His breathing hitched. "I've watched lots of videos that made me cringe, really heavy stuff. That's… that's not what I want."

Mark nodded. "You want kink, not hardcore BDSM." He smiled. "And you know what that is, don't you?" Dylan's vigorous nod was no surprise. "Then I think I have a good picture." He glanced at Dylan's crotch, noting the way the soft fabric jerked. "I'd better take care of that." Mark got onto his knees in front of Dylan, undid the tie around his waist, and pulled the robe aside to reveal his erect dick. Mark placed his hands on Dylan's thighs and spread his legs, to the sound of Dylan's harsh breaths. "I got that part right," he murmured.

"What?"

Mark leaned in. "You have a pretty cock." He licked the head, and relished the groan that rolled from Dylan's lips as Mark slowly took it into his mouth. He gave it a hard suck, then released it with a grin. "Tastes good too."

Then all talk ceased as Mark went about making Dylan shoot his load. He worked his own dick as he sucked and licked, alternating between swallowing Dylan's shaft to the root until Mark's nose was buried in his pubes, and licking a path from balls to slit, loving the shivers that rippled through Dylan as Mark brought him closer to orgasm, the noises that escaped him. And when he came, his cock throbbing on Mark's tongue, Mark swallowed every drop before licking him clean.

"My turn." Mark straddled Dylan's hips and tugged on his cock, his breathing as staccato as Dylan's as he neared his climax, until at last he shot over Dylan's chest, shaking as he came. When he was spent, he held Dylan's face in his hands and kissed him, overjoyed when Dylan held him close.

Mark didn't want to move. He stretched out on the couch, tugging Dylan to lie beside him, and covered them both with Mark's robe.

He had nowhere to be, and a beautiful man to hold. Falling asleep with Dylan in his arms felt…

Perfect.

Dylan had to admit, the day hadn't gone the way he'd anticipated. Napping on Mark's couch had been unexpected, but waking up to feel Mark curled around him…

He hadn't wanted it to end.

He lay there, imagining all the delicious things that would occur once Mark was awake. Except Mark's first suggestion was lunch in Ogunquit, and while Dylan would have preferred to stay indoors and naked, he had to admit Mark had the right idea.

Besides, he was starving.

What *had* surprised him was the choice of venue. Caffé Prego was a little Italian restaurant with an awning-covered patio and awesome food. Dylan had never eaten there, but he'd passed it enough times, casting longing glances at the tiny lights covering the trees in front of it. The place screamed romance, and even though it was the middle of the afternoon, eating there was all kinds of special.

Don't read too much into this, okay? It had become his mantra all through lunch. He told himself Mark had picked it because it looked nice, he'd read the reviews, he'd gotten a flier through the door, any reason Dylan could think of, apart from the one he wanted to be true. He'd lusted after Mark for so long, and now that he'd finally met him, the reality was so much better than anything Dylan had imagined.

He'd imagined a lot.

They'd shared shrimp cocktail, mushroom confit and eggplant caponata, and the entrees of Veal Parmesan and Chicken Saltimbocca had been to *die* for. Dylan had no idea how the day would end, but right then it was freakin' *perfect*.

They chose gelato for dessert, and while they were waiting, Dylan seized the moment to discuss what had been on his mind since their earliest conversation.

"Can I ask you something?"

Mark smiled. "Ask away."

"I know you talked about being pissed off when your stuff turns up on free sites, but is that the only thing that's making you rethink your career? You have a huge following. I see your posts, the comments…"

Mark took a drink of water. "It's not just that. Maybe life was easier with the studios. All I had to do was turn up and fuck. But now? There's everything else. Editing, promotion, updating and maintaining my website, social media…. That last one alone is a major ball ache. It's never-ending."

"I like your website. It's clean and easy-to-read. And I love your posts."

"I don't love the trolls," Mark responded gloomily. "Every day I have to remove comments from haters. It's a horrible task. I try not to let them get to me, but if anything, there are more of them out there with each passing day."

"I notice you don't do posts about your relationships." Dylan would have picked up on that pretty damn fast.

Mark sighed. "I'm not into fiction." When Dylan stared at him, he nodded. "My last relationship was four, five years ago."

"But…" Dylan frowned. "I don't get it."

"Remember I said I'd had boyfriends who couldn't cope with my career? Try every one of them."

Dylan was torn between sorrow for Mark's dating failures, and secret joy that he was single. "Maybe you should date another porn star. That might work out. At least they'd understand."

Mark huffed. "I did, back in my early twenties."

"What happened?"

"In a word, jealousy. He was bigger than me— and I'm not talking size, I'm talking following. I was just starting to get a name for myself. We even shot a few scenes together. Well, my fan base suddenly exploded into five figures, and he wasn't happy about it. I'd get a scene at a studio, and he'd make disparaging remarks about my screen partner. And it got worse. Then he met someone else—not in the industry—and I got kicked to the curb."

"Did you love him very much?"

Mark ran his finger around the rim of his water glass. "I can be honest about it now. Maybe love was too strong a word for what I felt. It took me a while to move on. Of course, it didn't help that I was seeing pics of him and his new bf, blissfully in love. I tried to avoid his posts, because I didn't want to read how happy he was, how he'd finally found love, because that just dumped shit all over everything we'd shared." He shrugged. "I learned my lesson. Don't date porn stars."

"Was there anyone else?"

Mark nodded. "My next boyfriend was a fan." He smiled. "Casey. I called him my stalker. It lasted a while, but… it wasn't meant to be. We're still friends at least. He's engaged, getting married next month." He peered at Dylan. "What about you?"

"After the episode with Della, I swore off relationships. I think my confidence took a beating."

"There's been no one since Casey. I guess I'm not built to fall in love."

Don't say that.

Dylan swallowed past the uncomfortable lump in his throat. "You don't know that. One of my friends—Seb—well, as long as I've known him, he's been this total… horndog." When Mark laughed, Dylan joined in. "Trust me, it fits. He was happy doing hookups, one-night stands… I thought I knew him, and then… This summer, he met someone. An older guy. And you know what? I don't recognize him anymore. Seb is in love, and it's such a good look on him. If he can find someone, there's hope for all of us."

Except that was skating on thin ice. Dylan knew he was crushing on Mark, but felt powerless to stop it, even though he knew what connected them was just sex.

Lord knew, he wanted it to be more than that.

Change the subject.

"I can understand why dating could be difficult for you."

Mark arched his eyebrows. "Yeah?"

Dylan nodded. "Guys see you perform on the screen, so they come with certain… expectations about what you'll do."

Mark snorted. "You've got that right. But there's something else."

"What?"

"They're going to bed with a porn star, so they think they need to *act* like a porn star. Over-the-top moans, nonstop noises…"

"Let me guess." Dylan grinned. "They say 'Fuck yeah' a lot."

Mark burst out laughing. "Exactly. They think that's what I want, and it *so* isn't. Give me a guy who lets me know he's into it without all the vocals, the dramatics…"

Dylan flushed. "Thanks for the tip."

"You're safe, judging by this morning." When Dylan raised his eyebrows, Mark smiled. "You weren't loud. But then again, I don't suppose it was your first such… experience."

"No, it wasn't, but it left all the other times in

the dust." Then he clammed up as a man approached their table with obvious hesitation, his gaze locked on Mark. "I think this is for you."

Mark glanced up, and stiffened for a second, before pasting on a smile. "Hey."

The guy smiled. "Excuse me for interrupting, but… are you Mark Roman?"

Mark nodded. "Guilty."

The man beamed. "I *thought* it was you. I kept watching you the whole time we were eating. Can I take a selfie with you?"

"Sure." Mark stood and went around the table to stand next to the guy, who held his phone out at arm's length. After a couple of attempts, he got a result that pleased him. Mark smothered a gasp as the guy gave him a brief hug.

"Thank you. Wait till I tell my friends. They'll be so jealous." With a nod to Dylan, he walked toward the steps that led down to the street.

Mark retook his seat. "Sorry about that. Occupational hazard."

"Do you get a lot of strange men hugging you?"

"Hugging me, pinching or smacking my ass… One guy asked if we could kiss for the selfie."

"And did you?"

Mark flushed. "Actually? Yeah. He was hot." Then he sighed. "But it's growing old." He cleared his throat. "Let's change the subject, because this will only bring me down." Mark peered at Dylan. "You've had an eventful day."

Dylan stilled. "Is it over?"

"Do you want it to be?"

He reined in the urge to yell 'Fuck no!' "No."

"Then why don't we go back to my place, and continue your... education?"

Chapter Fifteen

Getting to Mark's house was kind of a blur.

That might have had something to do with Dylan's head being elsewhere, and definitely not on the road ahead. What occupied his thoughts was that he knew what to expect—how many times had he watched Mark fuck someone? —and yet he didn't. Because the Mark who'd sucked him off was *nothing* like the man Dylan watched on his phone or laptop, and he was at a loss to understand why that should be.

Another conversation loomed—but not right then. All he could focus on was the imminent arrival of Mark's dick in his ass, because that was all he wanted. He'd waited long enough, damn it.

Mark coughed. "You did want to come back here, didn't you?"

Dylan blinked. They were on Mark's driveway, the engine was turned off, and Mark was grinning.

He unfastened his seatbelt and got out, Mark following with a chuckle. "Want to watch some TV? Shoot some pool? Unless there's something else you'd rather be doing."

Dylan waited while Mark unlocked the front door, then hurried inside. The moment Mark closed the latch, Dylan shucked off his jacket, kicked off his boots, and gave a little impatient whine as Mark took his time removing his outer wear and shoes.

"You're doing this deliberately, aren't you?" Dylan growled.

Mark gave him an innocent glance. "Doing what?" Then before Dylan could yell at him, Mark grabbed his hand and tugged him toward the bedroom. "Okay, dick-in-the-ass time."

"Wait, what?" Dylan's heart was thumping.

"That's what you want, isn't it?"

"Yes, but—"

"So what are we waiting for?" Dylan's breathing was ragged and harsh in the quiet room. Then Mark smiled, and Dylan went weak at the knees. Mark closed the gap between them. "You know where my bathroom is. Take your time. We've got the rest of the day to enjoy each other." His mouth met Dylan's, and Dylan sighed into the kiss.

"You really had me going for a second," he murmured when they parted.

"I told you. I'm going to be gentle. I want this to be good for you. But just so we're clear?" Mark's lips brushed his ear. "I can't wait to be inside you."

There went his heart again.

Dylan hurried into the bathroom, his mind in a whirl. *Okay. Let's do this.*

Mark left the toys where they were—there would be other occasions to play. All he needed was a towel, lube, and condoms. He caught the sound of running water from the bathroom, and smiled. He could recall prepping for his first anal scene, after receiving advice on the subject from his screen partner.

I was so nervous.

Mark knew exactly how he wanted to play this. He tingled with anticipation at the thought of exploring Dylan's lean, firm body, but it was more than that. He wanted Dylan to melt in his arms, to tremble with desire. Mark wanted Dylan to *soar.*

He had an idea that watching Dylan unravel would be something beautiful to behold.

The door opened, and Dylan emerged, his clothing gone, a towel wrapped around his hips. Mark held his arms wide. "Come here."

Dylan walked into them, and Mark pulled him close, his hands on Dylan's back. Their kiss was hesitant at first, but little by little, Dylan opened for him. The change in his breathing spoke of urgency and growing need, and Mark was aware of the hard length pressing against him.

He took a step back. "Undress me?"

Dylan smiled. "I can do that." He helped Mark out of his tee, then unbuttoned his jeans, kneeling as he lowered them to Mark's ankles. Mark's dick pointed at him, a solid arrow, pre-cum already beading at the slit. Dylan's breathing hitched, and he gazed up at Mark, his lips parted.

Mark cupped his cheek with one hand, and held his shaft with the other, aiming it at Dylan's mouth. "Is this okay?"

Dylan swallowed. "Yes. Am I okay to…?"

Mark nodded. "Good boy. Always ask. And I

wouldn't let you put your mouth on me if there was any risk."

His tongue on the head sent a thrill through Mark, and he moaned as Dylan lapped up the clear fluid. Dylan opened his eyes wide. "It tastes almost... sweet."

"Glad you like it, because there *will* be more." Mark knew there would be a constant stream of it by the time he was ready to glove up. He gasped as Dylan's warm mouth surrounded the head. "That's it. That feels good."

His words of praise brought a light to Dylan's eyes that made Mark's spirits soar. Dylan moved slowly, taking him in inch by inch, until three quarters of his cock had disappeared between Dylan's lips.

As blow jobs went, it was nothing like the fast, frenetic, swallow-it-to-the-root variety that Mark had grown accustomed to, and that made it all the better. Dylan's initial hesitancy, his burgeoning confidence, the little noises he made that told Mark he was enjoying the experience, the way Dylan's dick jerked as he sucked... Every part of it was bound up in a sense of joy as Mark let himself go, his hands resting lightly on Dylan's head, encouraging sounds tumbling from his lips as Dylan worked his shaft with lips and tongue.

Mark pulled free, unable to hold back his smile. "For a first-timer, that was pretty impressive."

"But... I couldn't take it all..."

Mark hoisted Dylan to his feet. "I didn't expect you to. Okay, I'd have been overjoyed if you'd swallowed me to the root, but I know *lots* of guys who can't accomplish that." He stroked Dylan's cheek. "Don't use porn as a measuring tool, okay? If you did that, you'd be forgiven for believing that every man has a nine-inch dick, astounding stamina, and not a gag reflex in sight." Dylan laughed. Mark kissed him. "Lie with me on the bed."

Dylan nodded, and then he chuckled. "You might want to take your jeans off first."

Mark bent to remove them before taking Dylan by the hand. He climbed onto the bed, tugging Dylan to stretch out beside him. Mark leaned over and kissed him, stroking Dylan's chest and abs before straying lower to cup his balls and give them a gentle squeeze. Dylan moaned into the kiss, his body rocking as he reached for Mark, exploring him with his fingers. His need proved infectious, and the heat between them intensified.

"Please," Dylan whispered.

"Tell me what you want."

"Would you… would you play with my hole?"

Mark grinned. "I thought you'd never ask. Roll onto your front and stick your ass in the air."

Dylan responded with a speed that was gratifying. He rested his forearms on the mattress and tilted his hips.

"Spread your legs for me, nice and wide."

Oh shit. Dylan did as instructed, his heartbeat racing. *I hope I did a good enough job. I hope it's squeaky*

clean. I hope—

All such thoughts fled when Mark spread his cheeks, and a warm, wet tongue licked a leisurely path over his hole. Dylan burst out laughing. "That tickles!"

Mark paused. "A ticklish hole? Good to know." Then Dylan felt the soft scrape of Mark's bearded chin through his crease, and he laughed again.

"You're doing that on purpose."

"Doing what?" Another rub, and Dylan was wriggling and laughing, unable to keep still.

And then everything changed when Mark pressed his tongue to Dylan's pucker.

Holy Mary, Mother of God.

"Fuck, baby, your ass tastes good," Mark said with a groan. Dylan's moan matched his as Mark grabbed Dylan's rigid cock and licked from head to hole. He stroked a finger over Dylan's pucker while he sucked on his dick, flicking the head with his tongue.

"Fuck, that feels…" Dylan shuddered, rolling his hips. The noises that poured out of Mark as he probed Dylan's hole with his tongue were almost… hungry. Then Dylan cried out when Mark took his balls into that warm mouth. "Oh God." He'd never imagined that could feel so good.

"Lie on your side," Mark urged him. When Dylan did so, Mark pushed his upper knee toward his chest, until his dick was pressing into the mattress, his hole exposed. Mark rubbed his fingers over it. "Does that feel good?"

"Oh yeah."

"I'm going to use lube while I play with this pretty hole, but I want you to do one thing for me."

"What's that?"

Mark leaned over and kissed the tip of Dylan's

nose. "Remember to breathe?" His eyes twinkled. Then he moved across the bed toward the nightstand.

Dylan heard the *click* of the lube bottle, then cool liquid trickled over his hole, followed by the warmth of Mark's fingers.

"You ever had anything in your ass before?"

"Maybe?"

Mark chuckled. "You can tell me." His fingers were gentle.

"I asked a girl to stick her finger in there. She said no. So when I was jerking once, I tried it with the tip of my finger."

"And what else did you put in there?"

Dylan craned his neck to stare at Mark. "How did you know?"

Mark grinned. "I'm getting better at reading you. So come on. Fess up."

"I… I might have used the handle of a hairbrush." Except he'd gone too fast, and the result had put him off trying such activities for a while.

Then he caught his breath as Mark eased a finger into him. "Jesus…"

"I bet that feels better than the hairbrush."

"Lube helps," Dylan admitted.

"Reach back and hold your cheeks open for me. That'll make it easier."

"I can manage one cheek. Is that enough?" Dylan grabbed it and spread himself wide. "Like that?"

"Perfect. Now, remember what I said about breathing." Mark kissed Dylan's hand, and then that finger slid deeper. "Oh, so tight. That's all the way in to the knuckle." He stilled inside him. "Just get used to how that feels. Let me know when you're ready for more."

Dylan drew in deep breaths, his head resting in the crook of his arm, his fingers digging into the flesh of his ass as he kept his hole stretched. "Lube *definitely* helps."

"Lube is our friend." Mark paused. "Can I try something?"

"I think *you're* driving this bus," Dylan observed. Then a wave of intense pleasure washed over him as Mark stroked inside him. "Oh dear *Lord*."

"That hit the spot," Mark murmured. He kept that up for a few minutes, until Dylan was aching for more. "Adding another." He ran his hand over Dylan's thigh. "Breathe, baby."

"You can keep doing that," Dylan said with a moan.

"What—using two fingers?"

"No—calling me baby." Some part of him *really* liked that. Mark leaned over again, and Dylan learned that being kissed while Mark fingered his ass took his pleasure to a whole new level. Mark added more lube, and then everything got hotter and slicker, until Dylan was writhing, wanting, *needing* more. Mark spooned up behind him, kissing his neck, his shoulders, and all the while moving two fingers in and out, taking his time.

When he added a third, it slid right in there like it fucking *belonged*.

Mark shifted lower, kissing Dylan's hip as he finger-fucked him. "That feel good?"

"Feels amazing."

"Can't tell you how hot it looks, my three fingers buried in your hole. You're taking them so well." Another kiss, this time to his waist. "Ready for my dick yet?"

Dylan twisted his upper body to gaze at Mark, his heart hammering. "Go slow, please?"

Mark kissed him, a lingering, sensual kiss that sent warmth flooding through him. "I promised I'd be gentle, didn't I?" Then he withdrew his fingers, reached behind him, and Dylan heard the crinkle of the condom wrapper.

"Lots of lube, right?"

Mark chuckled. "You know it." Another *click*, and then he knelt at Dylan's ass. "Hold it open for me, baby."

Dylan pulled on one ass cheek, Mark on the other, and then guided the head of his cock to kiss Dylan's stretched hole. "Gonna take this *so* slowly."

Dylan tried not to tense up, but *damn*, Mark had a thick dick. He took a couple of deep breaths, as Mark eased his way into Dylan, all the while gently stroking Dylan's chest, hip, and thigh. At last, he came to a stop.

"That's it. All the way inside you."

Dylan shivered. "Okay, that feels *so* much fatter than a hairbrush."

"Hopefully it feels better too." Mark gave a leisurely roll of his hips, and the resulting sensations threatened to overwhelm him. Mark stroked his leg. "Too much?" He stilled, and Dylan breathed a little easier.

"You're too far away," Dylan complained.

Mark smiled. "We can do something about that." He withdrew, and Dylan felt every inch of his cock as it left him empty. Mark slid his arm under Dylan's neck and shoulders, cradling Dylan to his chest as Mark entered him once more. "Is that better?"

"Much." Dylan turned his face toward Mark's, and their lips met in a soft kiss, Mark's dick fully sheathed in him.

Dylan had lost count of the number of times he'd imagined this moment, and it was *nothing* like his fantasies. Mark's hand cupped his cheek while they kissed, and to have him gaze into Dylan's eyes as he moved in and out of him was everything Dylan had hoped for, and yet so much more. Then Mark would stop, they'd kiss, and then he'd start again, as gentle as he'd promised, until Dylan knew he was ready for more.

"You can go a little faster now."

Mark pulled free of him. "On your back, sweetheart."

Dylan complied, spreading for him, and sighing when Mark was once again inside him. Mark cradled him once more as if he were something precious, and Dylan rested his heels on Mark's ass, feeling each thrust as Mark filled him again and again. He curled his toes, his breathing uneven as Mark picked up the pace.

"Touch yourself," Mark instructed.

"If I do that, I'll come." Dylan wanted it to last.

"Then come, and we'll do it all over again." Mark bit his lip. "I can't last much longer. Your ass feels too good."

Dylan had never felt so powerful.

He clung to Mark with one arm while he tugged on his dick, his body already tingling. Mark rocked in and out of him with short, quick thrusts, his breathing increasingly ragged. And when the wave hit, Dylan moaned, torn between the euphoria of his orgasm, and disappointment that the end had come so soon.

"Oh, Mark…" He shot hard, coating both his chest and Mark's, but Mark didn't slow. He pumped faster, his hips rolling, and Dylan held onto Mark's shoulders.

"Aw fuck," Mark groaned, and he stiffened. Dylan loved the steady throb of Mark's dick inside him, but to have Mark kiss him as he came was perfect. It was his turn to cradle Mark, kissing him as tremors coursed through him. And when at last Mark lay still in his arms, Dylan kissed his forehead, cheeks, and lips, hoping that would speak for him when words wouldn't come.

Mark sighed. "It's no good. I have to come out."

Dylan's heavy sigh echoed his. "Really?" He kissed Mark on the lips. "Can't we stay like this a while longer?"

Mark chuckled. "I have to dispose of something, remember?"

"Promise me we'll do this again."

Mark looked him in the eye. "You have my word." Then he sealed his promise with a kiss.

Dylan breathed him in, burning the moment into his memory. *I wanted you for so long, never dreaming you'd walk into my life. And now that you're here? I don't want to lose you.*

Chapter Sixteen

October 5

Dylan's shift was almost at an end, and he couldn't wait to get out of there. The day had dragged, one of those times when there had been few check-ins and no problems to solve. It didn't help that he'd been distracted since he'd strolled through the door that morning.

His head was full of Mark. In fact, it had been that way for a week.

Has it really been only a month since he walked into the hotel? It felt longer. The last seven days had taken on a pattern. His daytime was filled with work, but his nights were spent in Mark's bed. His roommates had started making jokes about the house not being a hotel. They wanted to know where he'd been, but Dylan was keeping quiet on that score. That had earned him all kinds of smutty remarks which he ignored.

Mark showed no signs of being unhappy with the present state of affairs. Each morning when Dylan hurried home to change for work, Mark had been the one to tell him dinner would be ready for him that evening, and Dylan figured if Mark had needed some alone time, he wouldn't have extended the offer.

More than his schedule had changed. Dylan had found his confidence.

Some nights, all they did was eat dinner and then curl up together on the couch and watch a movie, and that was fine by Dylan. It felt… comfortable. As soon as they slid between the sheets, however, the mood changed.

And speaking of between the sheets? Dylan was so hard, a cat couldn't scratch it.

"Mr. Martin."

Shit. Speaking of cats… Mr. Reynolds was as silent as one. "Yes, sir?"

The manager surveyed the reception desk. "Remind me of the date, please."

Dylan frowned. "Today's date, sir?"

Mr. Reynolds rolled his eyes. "Yes, today's date."

Dylan glanced at the calendar sitting right there in front of him. "October fifth, sir."

Mr. Reynolds nodded. "In which case, reception appears to be missing something."

Okay, he was confused as hell. "And what would that be, sir?"

The manager walked behind the desk, and kicked the cardboard boxes sitting under it.

Oh fuck. Dylan had been told to put out the Halloween decorations at the weekend, and it had slipped his mind. "I'll start working on it right now."

"Thank you. Just make sure it's done before you leave for the day."

He blinked. "I only have fifteen minutes until the end of my shift." Mr. Reynolds' eyes bulged. "But of course, I'll stay until it's done," he added hastily. *Shit.*

Mr. Reynolds cleared his throat, took one last look around, and strode through the lobby. Dylan waited until he was out of sight before pulling his phone from his pocket.

Mark answered within five rings. "I'll be seeing you in less than half an hour. What's so urgent?"

"You might need to reheat my dinner when I get there." Dylan explained the situation.

"Oops. Get the job done. I'll keep it warm for you." There was a pause. "Can you stay tonight?"

"That depends if you're asking me to."

Mark laughed. "Silly boy." He disconnected.

Warmth barreled through him. What they had going had a domesticated feel to it, and Dylan didn't mind that in the slightest.

A loud cough from the lobby had him reaching under the desk for the boxes.

Cobwebs, skeletons and spiders, oh my.

"Door's open," Mark yelled when the bell rang. He poked his head around the kitchen door. Dylan had obviously come straight from the hotel: he still wore his work clothes. Mark smiled. "Have I told you yet how good you look in a suit?"

Dylan kicked off his shoes. "I am *dead.*"

Mark went over to him and kissed him. "Aw, bad day? Did you get it all finished?"

Dylan nodded. He opened his mouth to speak, closed it, then tugged Mark closer. "Do that again."

Mark chuckled, but did as requested, loving Dylan's newfound confidence. "I missed you today," he murmured against Dylan's neck. Fuck, he smelled good.

Down boy.

Dylan looped his arms around Mark's neck. "Missed you too. In fact, it's your fault I forgot to put up the decorations."

"Mine?" Mark exclaimed with a hint of forced indignation.

Dylan gave a solemn nod. "I was thinking about you, and not about work. See? Your fault."

"Funny. I was thinking about you too, and yet *I* still managed to get stuff done."

Dylan snorted and removed his arms.

Mark smiled to himself. He'd been thinking about Dylan the whole time he'd jerked off for the camera, so it wasn't exactly a lie. "So, is the hotel Halloween-ready?"

"Yup. It's so full of creepy shit, you can't move. I even added spooky green spotlights for added creepiness. I thought the spider crawling out of the skeleton's mouth was a nice touch. It'll scare every little kid for miles." He sniffed. "Something smells fantastic."

"We're having meatloaf, mashed potatoes, green beans, and gravy." Mark had to smile when Dylan's face lit up. "Have I hit on another favorite?"

"Only if you've made enough meatloaf for sandwiches tomorrow."

Mark snorted. "Duh. Why didn't I think of that?"

"That was sarcasm, right?"

Mark kissed his forehead. "Take off your

jacket, take off your tie, undo your top buttons, and by the time you're more comfortable, I'll have a beer for you."

Dylan smiled. "You'd make someone a wonderful husband." Mark arched his eyebrows, and Dylan blinked. "Okay, did I say that out loud?"

He laughed and headed back to the kitchen. "You *have* had a long day." He went to the fridge and grabbed a couple of beers. The prospect of another evening in Dylan's company sent a slow tide of warmth spreading through him.

I could get to like this.

"Hey, you said *we're* having meatloaf. You've already eaten, haven't you?" Dylan called from the living room.

"Nope. I waited for you."

"Aw, you didn't have to do that." Dylan stood in the doorway, his feet bare, his waistcoat unbuttoned and his collar open.

Mark's dick reacted. Bare feet were sexy as fuck, and his open shirt hinted at the hair on Dylan's chest. With a supreme effort, he forced his mind back to the practical matter of feeding Dylan. "I wanted to. I like eating with you." Who was he kidding? Mark liked cooking for Dylan too. Having someone for dinner forced him to cook rather than buy TV dinners for one. The evening Dylan had come through the door and smelled freshly baked bread, Mark swore he'd drooled.

Mark had gotten into a new routine during the past week. Each morning when Dylan left for work, Mark recorded a solo session. Granted, his cum shots weren't as spectacular as previous ones, but that was because he'd already come once: getting rid of morning wood was infinitely more fun with two.

Dylan pulled out a chair and sat. "How was your day?"

"Productive. And I had an idea about what we could do after dinner." Dylan's eyes gleamed, and Mark guffawed. "Dirty boy. I was going to suggest we played some pool."

"Suppose I *want* to be a dirty boy?"

"Then you wait until bedtime," Mark said in a firm voice. The fact that Dylan was coming out of his shell pleased him no end.

"Spoilsport." Dylan's grin belied his words. "Maybe we should make it a contest."

"What did you have in mind?"

Dylan stroked his chin. "Hmm. Loser bottoms?"

Mark laughed. "I might have known sex would figure in it somewhere. Okay, deal. Because *you* are going to lose."

"Don't bet on it. I might have a secret weapon."

Mark's evening was shaping up to be a lot of fun.

Mark stood at the end of the pool table. "Have you played much pool?"

Dylan bit his lip. "Okay, about that… I haven't

actually played before."

"Wait… you said there's a table at the hotel."

"That's true," Dylan acknowledged. "But I also said I hadn't picked up a cue. There was a reason for that. I didn't want to embarrass myself."

"And you still think you're going to win our little contest?"

Dylan grinned. "Secret weapon, remember? But you're gonna have to teach me."

Mark shrugged. "I can do that." He picked up the cue. "Let's start with how you hold this. You grip it toward the base with your left hand, you rest your right on the table, making a V with your thumb, and that's where the cue sits." He demonstrated, sliding the cue back and forth.

"Like this?" Dylan copied him, except he stood close enough that Mark's nostrils were filled with the smell of his cologne, and that same warm, musky scent that lingered on his pillows long after Dylan had gone to work.

Mark arched his eyebrows. "If you take a step back, I'll show you how to break." Pride flushed through him at his ability to keep his voice even.

"Oh, sure." Dylan obliged with a grin. "Show me how it's done, then I'll show you what I've got." He gave a little thrust of his hips, and Mark was momentarily distracted by the bulge in Dylan's pants.

Oh, I get it. Suddenly, Dylan's *"secret weapon"* wasn't so secret anymore.

Two could play at that game.

Mark showed him how to stand, took aim, and sent the cue ball hurtling over the green felt, smashing into the balls and sending them in all directions. He straightened. "Okay, I didn't sink anything, so you go next."

Dylan took the cue and walked around the table to the cue ball. He bent over it, and Mark came up behind him. "Figure out which ball you're going to go for first," he said, stroking Dylan's back before sliding his hand lower to stroke his hip.

Dylan glanced at him for a second, then returned his attention to the balls. "Could I maybe hit the red one, to try and knock the purple one in?"

"You could," Mark mused, "but a better idea might be to try to knock it in with the eight-ball." He stood close enough that his crotch pressed against the back seam of Dylan's pants. "Remember how to hold the cue." He demonstrated again with his right arm, but this time he rocked gently against Dylan's ass.

Dylan coughed. "That's kinda… distracting."

"Aw, I'm sure you can do it."

Dylan aimed, shot, and sent the eight-ball toward the purple, giving it just enough forward momentum that it dropped into the corner pocket.

"Hey, you made it. Now it's your turn again." Mark pointed to the three. "Maybe try that one, straight down the line."

Dylan tried to position himself, but the angle was all wrong, so he changed it. Mark stood behind him, his hands on Dylan's hips. Dylan twisted to look at Mark over his shoulder. "You're doing it again."

"Doing what?" Mark took a step back, but as soon as Dylan took aim, he stroked his hip.

Dylan missed completely.

"Aw, too bad. My turn." Mark took the cue from him. "Now, let's see." He smiled. "I'm going to send the six-ball all the way to the far corner pocket." He rested the cue on his thumb, just as Dylan moved to the pocket, his crotch right in Mark's line of sight. Mark chuckled. "You might wanna stand someplace else. Otherwise, I might hit something vital." *And I know what you're doing.*

Damn him, it was working.

He pocketed the six, but missed the next one, so it was over to Dylan. "Let me try a combination shot."

Mark chuckled again. "Ooh, feeling confident, I see." He waited till Dylan had lined up for the shot, then snuck up behind him and placed his hands on Dylan's hips, doing a slow grind against his ass.

"Mark…"

He leaned in and whispered, "Hey, you've got your weapons, and I've got mine."

Dylan took a deep breath, aimed, and pocketed the ball. He grinned. "And I *still* managed to sink it." He surveyed the table.

"You could try to sink the three-ball," Mark told him, "but you'll need to lean right over the table."

Dylan tried it. "I can't reach it." Then he climbed onto the table, his ass pushed out as he aimed. "Hey, that works." He spread his knees, his elbows on the green felt as he contorted himself to take the shot. Once he'd sunk the three, he glanced over his shoulder. "See anything you like?"

Mark took one look at the fabric stretched tight over that firm ass, and growled. There was only so much temptation a man could take. Then he realized there was something in Dylan's back pocket.

Something unmistakably the shape of a condom.

"You little shit, you set me up."

Dylan wiggled his ass. "If you want it, take it."

He reached around Dylan, popped the catch on his pants, yanked the zipper, then pulled them down to reveal Dylan's bare ass.

Dylan's obviously *lubed* ass.

"When did you do this?"

"While you were loading the dishwasher." Then Dylan jerked his head toward the windows. "Hey, close the blinds. I don't wanna give your neighbors a free show."

"What, you didn't think to close them before we started playing?" Mark crossed the room and closed them, and when he turned back, Dylan was buck naked and leaning over the table, his weight on one hand while he worked his cock with the other, his legs spread.

Mark walked over to him, taking his time, stripping off his sweater and tossing it to the floor, then pushing his sweats down to his ankles and stepping out of them. "I don't think you've secreted a bottle of lube somewhere on your person," he teased.

Dylan coughed. "Side pocket."

"Side—" Mark peered into it, and found a couple of packets of lube. "Hey, these are from my work bag."

"The bottle wouldn't fit!" Dylan retorted. "Now will you hurry up and get that dick in my ass?"

Mark tore one of the packets, squeezed drops of the viscous fluid onto his fingers, and slid two into Dylan's glistening hole.

"Jesus, what happened to starting with one?"

Mark laughed. "I'm betting you've already had one in there—your own." He sawed them in and out, Dylan pushing back, impaling himself on them. "Okay, you've had enough." He reached into Dylan's pants and removed two condom wrappers. "Oh, *I* get it. Equal opportunities night?" He tore one, unfurled the rolled latex over his erect cock, and squeezed what was left of the lube along its length. Mark slid his dick through Dylan's crack before wedging it there while he reached around Dylan to tease his nipple.

"Not fair," Dylan moaned.

"Hey, you started this." Mark wrapped his arm around Dylan's shoulders, pulling him in, Dylan's back pressed to his chest as Mark kissed his neck. Dylan turned his head, demanding a kiss, and Mark claimed his mouth, grinding his shaft against Dylan's hole.

"You gonna fuck me, or keep teasing me?" Dylan gritted out.

Mark kissed his nape, and Dylan shivered. "Who's in charge here?" Mark demanded.

Dylan lowered his head to the table, his weight on his elbows. "You are, sir."

"Good boy." Mark delivered a sharp smack to Dylan's ass cheek.

"For now," Dylan murmured. He rolled his hips, and Mark's dick slid up and down over his hole.

Mark couldn't wait a second longer.

He teased Dylan's hole with the head of his cock, then pushed, sighing as tight heat sucked him in. "Oh yeah," he whispered.

"Don't you mean, 'Fuck yeah'?" Dylan groaned as Mark bottomed out. "That's it. Now fuck me."

Mark put his hands on Dylan's waist and moved slowly at first, sliding in and out with a roll of his hips. When Dylan pushed back to meet his thrusts, Mark knew it was time to change the pace. He drove his dick all the way home, and Dylan's moans punctuated every glide of his shaft.

"God, I love that cock," Dylan said with a gasp as Mark buried his dick in Dylan's ass.

Mark chuckled, his hips pumping. "Whatever happened… to that shy boy… I met in the hotel? … The one who couldn't… look at me without… turning a pretty shade of red?"

Dylan twisted to gaze at him over his shoulder. "You fucked the shy right out of him." He groaned when Mark went deep. "You complaining?"

"I liked that shy boy." Mark came to a halt, and tugged Dylan into an upright position. He kissed his neck, loving the shiver that rippled through Dylan. "But I like this sexy man even more." Then he pushed Dylan down onto the table, placed his hands on the small of his back, and went to town on his hole, hips snapping as he fucked him.

"Harder," Dylan demanded, and Mark gripped his hips, yanking him back onto his dick, their bodies colliding with a *smack*. Dylan spread his arms wide, hooking his fingers into the side pockets and holding on as Mark slammed into him. "Oh my God. Oh fuck. Fuck."

"That's what you asked for, wasn't it? To be fucked?" When Dylan reached back to grab Mark's leg, Mark hoisted him upright again, his arm wrapped around Dylan's chest as he kissed him with a ferocity that had come out of nowhere. Dylan covered Mark's hand with his own, pushing back onto Mark's cock while they kissed, fucking himself on it. Then he leaned forward, his hands flat to the table, and changed gear, rocking slowly to take every inch of Mark's shaft. It was an exquisite sensation, but not enough.

Mark wanted to be balls-deep in that hot ass.

"Lift your leg up," he demanded. "Put your foot on the table."

"Gymnastics now?" Dylan didn't hesitate, however, and the motion stretched him wide open. Mark filled him to the hilt, holding onto Dylan's hips as he drove into him.

"We've got two condoms, remember?" Dylan gasped between thrusts.

Mark stilled inside him, his arms around Dylan's body, holding him close. "How do you want me?"

Dylan turned his head. "On the table, on your back." When Mark eased out of him, Dylan laid a hand on Mark's thigh. "Don't remove the condom. I'm not finished with you yet." Mark laughed, and Dylan grinned. "Hey, I did warn you I'd be taking charge, didn't I?"

Mark was liking this confident Dylan more and more.

He got onto the table, his ass resting on the edge, one knee drawn up to his chest. Dylan unrolled the condom down his hard shaft, then rubbed over Mark's hole with slick fingers. "I've thought about doing this so many times."

"Why didn't you just say something? You know I'm versatile." He stifled a moan when Dylan penetrated him with two fingers. "Oh, that's good."

Dylan locked gazes with him. "I don't really know. I love it when you're inside me. I guess now felt... right." He smiled. "Your hole is so tight around my fingers."

"It'll feel even better when my body's wrapped around your cock."

Dylan didn't want to wait anymore. He withdrew his fingers, brought the head of his dick to press against Mark's hole, and gave a leisurely push, watching as whatever air captured under the latex was squeezed out by the tightness of Mark's channel. "Oh fuck, that feels..." He bottomed out, leaning forward to kiss Mark's raised knee. "Amazing." Then he straightened, gazing at his glistening shaft spearing in and out of Mark's body.

It was mesmerizing.

"I could look at that all day," he murmured.

"You don't have to go slow," Mark commented, reaching for the side of the table.

Dylan smiled. "That's good, because I don't want to." He gripped Mark's knee and picked up speed, driving in and out of his ass with a fluid motion that felt *so fucking good* on his cock. Then he paused. "Something I need to do." He spread Mark's legs, hooked his arms under Mark's knees, rolled his ass up off the edge, and leaned over to kiss him as he slid all the way home. "That's better."

"Much better." Mark groaned. "That angle is fucking perfect."

Dylan settled into a rhythm, alternating between filling Mark's ass with long thrusts and kissing him, while Mark's latex-encased dick bounced with each impact, losing none of its hardness. Now and then he'd slow to a crawl to watch his shaft disappear into Mark's body, Mark's hole sucking him right in. He wanted to laugh from the sheer joy of it all.

Mark reached for his cock and gave it a pump, and suddenly Dylan knew exactly how he wanted to come. "Can I ride you?" he asked, pulling free of Mark's body.

Mark grinned and shuffled farther back along the table. "All aboard." Dylan climbed onto it and straddled Mark's hips, reaching behind him to swipe lube over his hole. He guided Mark's cock into position, and both moaned when he sank onto it, his ass cheeks meeting Mark's groin.

"Fuck, that feels so good." Dylan tugged at the condom on his own dick, tossing it to the floor. He curled his fingers around his shaft and began to ride, bouncing up and down on Mark's thick cock, using his legs to lift himself.

"I think… fucking on the pool table… definitely counts as kinky," Mark said between pants.

"You like it?" Dylan rode him a little harder, his hips bucking.

Mark stared at him with wide eyes. "Like? No, I fucking *love* it. Keep that up and you're gonna make me come real fast."

"I'm close too," Dylan confessed. With one hand on Mark's shoulder and the other gripping his shaft, he bounced harder and faster. "Jesus, you're deep." He let go of Mark and leaned back, holding onto the edge of the table as he sank onto Mark's cock over and over, his own dick bobbing and swaying. All too soon, he felt that prickle of electricity telling him the end was in sight, and he grabbed his cock, working it.

"Shoot on me," Mark demanded, his breathing

harsh and loud.

Dylan nodded, moving his hand faster. He stilled as he came, his cum spattering Mark's chin and neck. Each jolt sent another spike of pleasure through him, and before it had finished, Mark planted his feet on the green felt, tilted his hips, and slid in and out of him, gathering speed. Their mingled groans filled the air as Mark filled the latex, and Dylan focused on that throb inside him.

He bent down to kiss Mark on the lips, and Mark enfolded him in his arms. Dylan buried his face in Mark's neck, still riding the waves of contentment that coursed through him.

"I never knew pool could be so exhausting," Dylan murmured.

"We haven't finished the game yet."

Dylan jerked his head up. "You want us to keep playing?"

Mark grinned. "Certainly. I've got a contest to win, remember?" He reached down and grabbed Dylan's ass. "So you'd better get used to this feeling, because this hole will be mine again before the night is through."

Dylan reckoned this was one game he'd be happy to lose.

They climbed off the table, and Mark went in search of a towel. Dylan stared at the spots of cum on the felt. *Oops.* Mark would have a permanent reminder of their first game.

Dylan didn't want to think that one day there might be a last game. Right then, whatever it was they had going felt like some blissful dream, one he didn't want to wake up from.

Chapter Seventeen

October 9

Mark glanced at the notepad beside his laptop. Requests for appearances, hosting a party, a photo shoot, modeling underwear… Okay, so it was all work, but just *looking* at the list exhausted him. He'd spent the morning updating the website and sharing links to his latest video. Part two of the gang bang session had gained even more likes than part one, and he was getting a ton of messages asking for more of the same, not to mention requests from guys who wanted to film with him, meet him, or just fuck him.

At least they're upfront about it.

When his phone buzzed with a text from Joey, he wasn't surprised in the slightest.

Have you seen those numbers? SWEET.

Mark clicked *Call.* "Yes, I have, and no, I'm not going to do another."

"Seriously? You haven't changed your mind?"

If anything, the past two weeks had solidified the decision. "I'm done."

"But…"

Mark sighed. "You want to hear something that will shock the hell out of you? I haven't worked out for two weeks." Not that he'd been entirely inactive—sex made for great cardio.

There was silence for a moment. "Excuse me,

but I think I got a wrong number. Who is this?"

He chuckled. "Yeah, I know."

"And how do you feel about that?"

"Guilty as hell. But it's also made me see things more clearly. Up till now, I've had this constant need to stay in shape. You've seen me at the gym, right? Well, I had an… epiphany. I realized I wasn't working like a demon on the treadmill and the rowers and the weights for *me*—I was doing it all for the cameras, the fans. Christ, I can't remember the last time I thought about food without going through some mental rigmarole, deciding how I was going to work it all off later."

"I had no idea."

"Yes, you did," Mark retorted. "We all do it. Just visit any porn site and take a good hard look at the models. All those lean, toned, beautiful bodies… And what message does it send? Right now, there's some young guy looking at my picture and saying 'Why can't I look like that?' And there's probably nothing wrong with how he looks—he's just got it into his head that this is how guys are supposed to be."

Joey coughed. "There are a load of daddy bears out there who don't give a shit how they look."

"And more power to them, but I don't want to be a daddy bear, okay?"

Another pause. "You were gonna tackle that whole work-life balance thing, remember? The last time we spoke, you were planning on discovering Maine with some straight guy."

"Yeah, well, a lot's happened since then. I haven't seen all that much of Wells, let alone Maine, but I *have* seen a lot of him. And he's not straight—

he's bi."

Joey chuckled. "Okay, this is sounding better. Is he gonna stick around?"

God, I hope so. They were taking things one day at a time, but only because Mark was too scared to suggest they might make the situation a bit more permanent. *Been there, done that, got the scars to prove it.* "Right now, I don't know, is the honest answer. But I *am* serious—I'm going to find another way to make money."

Joey sighed. "I hear ya. What with the bar, and the promo side of porn, I'm running out of hours in the day. If all I had to do was tend bar and fuck for the camera, I'd be sweet. But it's everything else. I can't remember the last time I brought my site up-to-date. I think it was a year ago, and that ain't no way to run a railroad. Maybe I need to pay someone to do it for me."

Mark understood him all too well. "Fucking is the easy part—it's everything else that takes up the time."

"Yeah, and you don't have a job like I do." He paused. "This guy… he's important, isn't he?"

"I get the feeling he could be, yeah."

"Then don't let go of him, you hear? You hold onto him. Does he know about the porn?"

Mark chuckled. "Oh yeah."

"And he's still around? He's a keeper."

That pretty much summed up Mark's feelings too. *I don't want to lose him.*

Now all he had to do was find out if Dylan wanted to stay.

Dylan shoved his dirty clothing into the washer and closed the door. Mark had offered to do his laundry, but Dylan felt that was a step too far. Mark had his own life, and Dylan was already taking up a lot of it. What worried him was that at some point this fragile bubble surrounding them was going to burst.

Not yet. Please, God, not yet.

Dylan had forced himself to spend his day off at home. He told himself he couldn't be expected to clean up shit he hadn't created in the first place, and seeing as it was mostly his roommates' messes, they couldn't complain that he hadn't been around. That didn't stop him from tidying while they were at work. Besides, he'd feel better about going to Mark's that evening if he'd gotten stuff done at home.

Except it didn't feel like a home. To Dylan's way of thinking, a home was where you belonged, where you felt comfortable, and right then?

Mark's place felt more like home than this ever had.

His phone vibrated, and he peered at the screen. It was a text from Levi.

Have you dropped off the planet, or is work keeping you real busy?

Yet another thing to give him a major case of the guilts. *When did I last speak with any of the guys?* There had been that one call from Seb and Marcus, but that had been it since Aaron's BBQ. Dylan went into the kitchen, poured himself a glass of juice then retreated to his room. Once he'd gotten comfy on the bed, he called Levi.

"Hey. I'm still here, still breathing."

"I figured you must be snowed under at work. I was starting to get worried, so I checked. When I realized it wasn't just me, and that no one had heard from you for a while…"

Dylan bit back a sigh. "I… I've had a lot going on, that's all."

"Such as?"

"I'm figuring things out." That was the truth, wasn't it?

There was a pause before Levi spoke. "Are you okay?"

Dylan wasn't sure he could answer that question, so he went with evasion. *I've been doing that the whole time I've known these guys.* "I'm good. Let's talk about you. How's work?"

"I'm loving this whole working-at-home deal. I get time to do stuff for Grammy, spend time with my friends…" He chuckled. "If you believe the media, we've all become tech-savvy, but I have to tell you, there are *tons* of people out there who don't have a clue when it comes to technology. Then there are those who do, but have no time to do anything with it. All of which is good news for me, so while there are companies out there who want to pay people like me to maintain their sites, promote them on social media, I'm a happy bunny."

Dylan was sort of listening, but Levi's voice had morphed into a familiar, comforting pattern that washed over him, some of his words making it through to Dylan's brain but the rest were definitely falling by the wayside.

Then he realized he wasn't being fair.

I've hung around them all my life, asking questions, soaking up their friendship, and never really letting them in. They're good to laugh with, I love their company, but they don't have a clue what makes me tick.

Maybe it was time to change that. He didn't have to do it all at once. One person at a time— starting with Levi.

"Dylan? You're worrying me again."

"I was just… debating whether or not I should mention something." Except the internal debate was over, and he'd made up his mind.

"Is it important?"

Dylan smiled to himself. "You might say that."

"Look, if there's stuff you want to share, I'm here for you." The sincerity in Levi's voice rang clear. "And it'll go no further, not if you don't want it to."

He breathed deeply. "I realized something about myself—actually, it's more a case that I admitted the truth about something I've been denying for a long while now."

Another pause. "Christ, I have goose bumps. Just *tell* me, for God's sake."

Moment of truth.

"I… I'm bisexual."

The silence that ensued sent his heart rate into the stratosphere.

"Seriously? Newsflash for ya. Some of us have never been completely convinced you were straight."

Tears pricked the corners of his eyes, and a giddiness stole over him. "Really?"

Levi chuckled. "I always figured there was something behind all that curiosity. But I have to ask… did something happen to bring about this realization?" Before Dylan could respond, Levi caught his breath. "Oh my God. You've met someone. You have, haven't you?"

"Yes, but—"

"Well, spill. I guess we're talking a guy, what with the whole 'I'm bi' bombshell."

Dylan sighed. "His name's Mark, I met him just before Labor Day, and right now I have no fucking clue where this is going. All I know is, I'm happier than I've been in a long time."

"I'm glad. I always thought you needed a bit of that."

Dylan's breathing quickened. "What… what do you mean?"

"As long as I've known you, there's been… I don't know, *something*… that hung over you, like a cloud. Something you were hiding. But I figured you'd tell us, if we needed to know."

The tears he'd wiped away welled once more, and Dylan's throat seized.

"Hey, it's okay." Levi's voice was soft. "Can you tell me about him?"

Dylan swiped his fingers across his cheeks. "He's older than me—he's thirty-five—and he's amazing."

"Nine years' difference? Sweet." He paused. "And everything's good so far?"

Dylan knew where Levi was coming from. "Good doesn't cover it. Put it this way… I used to think Seb was unusual, that no one could be *that* horny all of the time. Now I know different. He's probably normal."

Levi burst into laughter. "Well, *that* explains why no one has heard from you. Color me jealous. You're having *loads* of fun, aren't you? Pun most definitely intended."

Mark was the bright spot on Dylan's horizon. That morning he'd glanced at the naked girl calendar Greg had pinned to the kitchen wall, and a cold wave had flushed through him. His dad's text had sat in his inbox, unread, but he couldn't ignore it any longer.

"Dylan? There's something else, isn't there?"

He'd gotten this far…

"My mom is fifty this Sunday. There's a party." At least, he assumed that was what the text was about.

"You don't sound all that enthusiastic. And… you just surprised the hell out of me."

"How?"

"You *never* talk about your family, not even when we were kids. We all keep coming up with theories for why that was, but none of us would push you on it. We figured you must've had your reasons."

"I didn't want to drag you guys into a toxic mess."

Levi's breathing hitched. "Christ. Oh dude… That bad?"

"Bad enough that I don't wanna talk about it."

"I hear ya. But… this party… do you have to go?"

"Yeah. But it's one day, right? I can put up with it for one day." He hoped.

"Now I don't know whether to be happy for you, or miserable as fuck." A pause. "You *are* coming to my Halloween party, aren't you?"

Dylan smiled. "I put in for that weekend off as

soon as you sent the text about it."

"Great. Bring Mark."

"What?" Dylan's heartrate climbed again.

"Bring him. You don't need to tell everyone who he is—just say he's a friend in need of a good party, okay? And *I* won't tell them."

"Jesus, Levi… It's a little more complicated than that." Such as, walking into a party with a gay porn star on his arm. Because if *Marcus* knew who Mark was, then Levi, Seb, Finn, Joel, Ben… they might know too.

"At least think about it?"

"Okay, I'll think about it." He could promise that much, right? Besides, Mark might not want to go.

Worse than that was the prospect that Mark might not want to stay in Dylan's life, and Dylan wasn't ready to think about that yet.

Since the moment Dylan had walked through his front door, Mark hadn't been able to shake the suspicion that something was wrong. Maybe it was the air of distraction that hung around him, the feeling that he was half-listening to Mark talking about his day, the noncommittal responses about how Dylan had spent his day off.

When Dylan showed no enthusiasm for a plate of mac and cheese, Mark wasn't prepared to stay silent any longer.

"What's wrong?"

Dylan jerked his head up from his plate. "Hmm?"

Mark wiped his lips, then put the napkin aside. "I don't know where your head is right now, but it's not here. And since when don't you wolf down my mac and cheese? So why don't you tell me what's worrying you? And don't tell me it's nothing, because I'll just call bullshit."

Dylan swallowed. "There's someplace I have to be Sunday, and I don't wanna go there."

Mark stilled. "Where?"

"My mom's birthday party."

Mark winced. "Do you have to go?" The loss of appetite had been a bit of a giveaway, now he thought about it. Dylan had been the same at Wonder Mountain, when he'd finally spilled.

"Unfortunately, yes. It's her fiftieth."

There was no way Mark wanted him walking into that place alone. "I'll come with you."

Dylan's eyes widened. "Fuck no. I don't want you anywhere near them." The tremor in his voice shook Mark.

He covered Dylan's hand with his. "You don't need to tell them *anything*, do you hear? You just walk in there, smile, kiss your mom on the cheek, hand over the gift, then do whatever you need to do to walk out of there with your soul intact." He squeezed Dylan's hand. "Think of me. Think of us, in bed. Or on the pool table. That'll put a smile on your face."

Dylan chuckled, but it sounded forced. "You're right. They don't need to know jack."

He smiled. "And then you come straight here,

and I'll make it all go away, I promise."

"Yeah? How you gonna do that?"

"Make love till dawn, if that's what it takes." He could be honest with himself. Sure, they both enjoyed a good, hard fuck, but late at night, when he was rocking in and out of Dylan's body, his movements as gentle and slow as their kisses…

It was as far removed from fucking as it was possible to get.

"I'm gonna hold you to that," Dylan said quietly.

"And I'm going to hold *you*, all night long." *And never let you go.*

Given half a chance.

October 11th

"Dad says you're still a supervisor," Livvy said as she and Dylan helped themselves to a slice of the birthday cake.

Lord, his sister was as bad as his parents. "'Still'?" None of his sisters had ever been remotely interested in his job.

Livvy shrugged. "I guess if you don't have the smarts to progress further than that, at least you have a job."

His stomach was as hard as a board, and he didn't think he'd manage to force down a single mouthful of cake. It would probably stick in his throat.

Dylan put the plate on the table. "I'm going to get a drink."

"Yes, I'd love one. Thanks for asking," she fired at him as he walked away.

Dylan ignored her and went into the dining room where his dad had set up a small bar. The house was full of relatives Dylan hadn't seen for years, and it had to have taken a lot of organizing. A fact his dad had been keen to stress the minute Dylan had removed his jacket. There were aunts, uncles, cousins…He'd gotten polite nods and smiles, some perfunctory greetings, but apart from that, everyone seemed to have formed themselves into little cliques.

Except me. Where do I fit in?

He already knew the answer to that—he didn't. He never had.

Dylan debated sticking to something soft, or pouring himself a glass of the champagne his dad had opened. It didn't matter that he'd avoided the hard stuff all evening—someone was bound to make a comment, although how he'd made it this far without the buffering effect of alcohol, he would never know.

Fuck it.

Dylan filled a glass to the brim with champagne, and the bubbles tickled his nose as he took a large mouthful of the golden liquid.

"Glad you could join us." Mom held out her empty glass.

Dylan filled it. "Hey, you're only fifty once, right?"

"Does that mean we won't see you again until the next big birthday? Because that's the only thing that seems to get you here. Of course, I realize we're not as important as those friends of yours."

He sipped his champagne, trying to quell the urge to respond.

"So, are you seeing anyone?" She gave him a hard stare. "Not that I'd expect you to tell me if you were. You never brought a girl home, not once. And looking at the… company you keep, well, I guess it's to be expected."

He blinked. *What the fuck?*

"We've been saying it for years," Mom continued. "You associate with those types, and people will make assumptions." Dad joined them, not that Dylan was in the least bit surprised. He'd known it was coming.

Fuck it. Dylan was done being polite. "Excuse me?"

Dad rolled out a heavy dramatic sigh. "Don't waste your breath, dear. Dylan has been kind enough to grace us with his presence, so let's not get him all riled up. Heaven knows how long it will be before he shows up again if we do that."

Jesus, it was as if he wasn't even there, the way they talked over him. Anyone listening to them would've believed *he* was the one being too sensitive.

Then he realized they would never change, that every visit would be just like the previous one. *Why would I want to subject myself to this… torture?* He felt numb, his limbs heavy. *Why should I? If this is all I'm going to get from them… more of the same…* Maybe it was time to accept that Levi and the rest of his friends had been more of a family to him than his own flesh and blood.

It was also time to burn some bridges.

Dylan put his glass down. "Okay… 'those types'. If you mean some of them are gay, then don't be coy, come right out and say it. But before you do, I should state for the record that I'm not gay." His mom opened her mouth, but Dylan wasn't about to let her get a word in. "Actually, I'm bisexual. You know what that means, right? I like girls *and* boys. Except I happen to have fallen for a man, not a boy, and he makes me very happy." He ignored their synchronized strangled gasps. "I don't know if it will last—I hope so, but who knows what the future holds in store for me? I do know one thing for certain—even if I lose him, even if these weeks are all we get, I'll have been happier with him than I've been in this family for a long, long time. And if I have to walk away from my family and create a new one with people who accept me as I am, who appreciate everything I do, and who support me unconditionally, then that's what I'll do. In fact…" He swallowed, then lifted his head high. "I'm doing it. Right now. Don't bother to see me out, I know the way." And without another word, he marched into the hallway to grab his coat.

He should've known it wouldn't be *that* easy.

The dining room door closed behind him. "You think this is a surprise? You think we're shocked?" That was his dad. "You think we haven't seen this coming ever since you told us what they were like?" He scowled. "It's no surprise. You lie with dogs, you get fleas."

He spun around to meet his dad's hostile gaze, his heart hammering. "So you think they *infected* me, is that it? Really? It doesn't occur to you that this is how I am? How I've always been?" Then the door opened, and his mom joined them, her face flushed. Dylan pushed out a groan. "I'm not gonna stand here and argue with you, because it'd just be a waste of breath. So this is me, getting out." He grabbed his jacket, opened the door, and left the house that had never been a home.

It wasn't until he unchained his bike from the gatepost that he realized he was too shaky to ride it. His fingers trembling, he reached into his pocket for his phone, and found Mark's number. As soon as the call connected, he blurted out, "Please, can you come get me?"

"Tell me where you are. I'm on my way out the door." Dylan rattled off the address. "Okay. I'm coming."

"Thank you." Dylan disconnected, then walked his bike down the driveway to the street. He lowered it to the ground before sitting on the low wall, his head in his hands.

I can't believe I did that. He felt sick, his stomach roiling, but there was also a growing sense of relief. *It's over. I don't have to go back there ever again.* A brief pang of guilt speared through him. *It should never have come to this. No one should be forced to make such a decision.*

But he'd made it, and with each passing moment, his resolution solidified.

He'd done the right thing.

A car screeched to a halt a few feet away, Mark flung open the door and hurried over to him, the engine still running. "Are you all right?" He helped Dylan to his feet.

Dylan didn't care anymore that someone in the house would see. He buried his face in Mark's neck. "I am now."

Mark held him in silence, then kissed his

cheek. "Let's get out of here."

He picked up his bike, and Mark popped the trunk. Once it was safely stowed, they got into the car, and Mark pulled away from the curb.

Dylan didn't glance back.

Chapter Eighteen

Mark's leftover meatloaf had hit the spot, but the cuddles on the couch fed a different kind of hunger.

I needed this. What shocked him was the degree of need. *It wasn't just a line, was it? I've fallen for him.* It hadn't been merely an admission to his family, but to himself.

"Feeling better?"

Dylan nodded. "Feeling calmer." He craned his neck to meet Mark's gaze. "Can I stay tonight?" *Please say yes.* He wanted to fall asleep in Mark's arms, to hold onto him throughout the night. Right then he wouldn't think about the future—he'd take whatever he could get in the present.

Mark frowned. "You really think I'd let you go home after that?" He tugged Dylan close and kissed the top of his head. "Now I need coffee. Want some?"

"Please."

Mark got up and went into the kitchen. Dylan checked his phone: there were no messages from anyone in his family. He was pretty sure they wouldn't be silent for long, however. Then a notification popped up, and he had to smile. "You've been busy while I was gone."

"Huh?" Mark stuck his head around the door. "Did you say something?"

Dylan held up his phone. "I said you've been busy. Your latest video?"

Mark smiled. "Yeah, I finally got around to uploading the third part of that gangbang. That's all of it." He retreated back into the kitchen.

Dylan opened the link and clicked *Play*. He'd already seen parts one and two, and they'd had him reaching for a glass of cold water and his lube. He watched for a couple of minutes before Mark came in with the coffee cups. Dylan paused it with a sigh. "You work with some gorgeous men."

Mark regarded him with raised eyebrows. "Sure. Some of them are drop-dead gorgeous. Most of them couldn't hold a candle to you."

He blinked. "Me? I'm nothing special."

Mark sat beside him. "Okay, two things. We never see ourselves as others see us. And a person's personality, what's on the inside, is just as important as what's on the outside." He leaned over and kissed Dylan on the lips. "You, sweetheart, are beautiful, inside *and* out."

No one had ever spoken to him like that, and it shocked him into silence.

"You don't get to see what *I* see." Mark gave him a thoughtful glance. "And maybe it's time you did." He stood, then took hold of Dylan's hand. "Come with me."

He led Dylan toward the bedroom. "You know, if you wanted to go to bed early," Dylan teased, "you could've just said."

"You need to bear with me, okay?" Once inside, Mark went to the closet and returned with two tripods.

"What are you doing?" Dylan demanded.

Except it was obvious as Mark set one up at the side of the bed, and another at the foot of it. Then he left the room, returning with two tablets that he clamped to the top of the tripods. Dylan's stomach clenched. "You're… you're not going to film us…"

Mark removed his phone from his pocket and waved it. "Uh-huh."

"You can't… I mean, I don't want anyone seeing me…"

Mark walked over to him and kissed him. "Trust me. This is just for me, okay? No one else will see it—except you when I'm done with it."

"Why would I want to watch myself?"

"Because you might learn something." Mark placed his phone on the bed, then drew Dylan to him. "Now, I want you to forget about the cameras, and—"

"You're kidding, right?" Dylan gestured to them. "They're kinda hard to ignore."

"Try? For me?"

Dylan gave the tablets another glance. "Making no promises, all right?"

"Thank you." Then Mark was kissing him, undressing him, making him hot, and Dylan couldn't think straight anymore.

He couldn't point to the moment when he stopped thinking about the cameras and let himself go: it had come and gone without him noticing. He hadn't even minded when Mark picked up his phone to record the slide of his dick in and out of Dylan's ass, or a close-up of Dylan's face while Mark had rolled his hips, filling him over and over again. And by the time he coated Mark's face with his cum, he'd forgotten completely—until Mark got off the bed to stop the recording. Then he returned to Dylan and held him while they kissed.

Dylan laid his head on Mark's chest. "We could've waited until it was time for bed. Not that I'm complaining." He stroked Mark's belly.

Mark chuckled. "I have things to do before then." He kissed Dylan's forehead, then got off the bed.

"Are we done?" Dylan asked with amusement. "Show's over?"

"I need some time on the laptop, so if you want a shower, you have it all to yourself."

Dylan pulled a face. "What if I don't want it to myself?"

Mark laughed. "You know what happens when we try to shower together."

"That's what I was hoping for." Dylan gasped when Mark smacked his bare ass. "Hey."

Mark gave him an innocent stare. "Hey nothing. It's on your list." Then he took the tablets and his phone, and padded naked out of the bedroom.

"Close the blinds!" Dylan hollered.

"Already did," Mark yelled back.

Dylan headed into the bathroom and took the opportunity to have a long shower. By the time he emerged from Mark's bedroom in one of Mark's robes, he felt human again.

I left home a long time ago. All I did today was finish the process. All evening, he'd asked himself if it could have gone any other way, or if the split had always been inevitable. *Would they have changed over time?* He thought it unlikely. They were too set in their ways, and their attitudes were ingrained in them.

I need people around me who lift me up, not drag me down. Then he smiled, a warmth stealing through him that had nothing to do with the shower.

Mark lifts me up.

He went into the living room to find Mark sitting on the couch, still naked, the laptop balanced on his thighs. He patted the seat cushion beside him. "Sit here. I want to show you something."

Dylan chuckled. "Just so you know? This feels weird." He joined Mark on the couch.

"I know, but I want you to see yourself as I see you. I think it might surprise you." Then he hit the Play button. "I've edited it so it looks like one of my videos."

It was like watching a stranger. The sounds that poured out of him, the way he arched his back as Mark entered him, the way he moved as he rode Mark's dick… And then there was the expression on his face when Mark came inside him, the light in his eyes, his face…

"Do I really look like that? *Sound* like that?"

Mark hit Pause. "You know how people hate listening to themselves? Same principle. But I could put that online, and it wouldn't look out of place among all my other content."

"Seriously?" Mark nodded. "But you won't, will you?" Dylan paled.

"No, I wouldn't do that, not unless you asked

me to."

"I'm telling you now. I will *never* want that."

"And that's fine. Hey." Mark squeezed his arm. "You have a position of responsibility in the hotel. Why would I risk that?"

Dylan gazed at the screen. "Can I ask you something?"

"You say that a lot, you know. And yes, you can ask me anything."

"When you're with me… when we're in bed—or wherever—is it… real?"

Mark had to think for a moment what he meant. Then he saw the light. "Remember when you first told me what you wanted? The intimacy you saw on the screen? Well, when I'm shooting porn, it's a performance. I perform for the camera, and for the audience who'll eventually see it. So I have to take everything into account. The camera angles, for one, because guys want to watch my dick slide into someone's ass. Rimming… don't get me started. It's impossible. Viewers want to watch my tongue in some guy's hole, but to do that, it means coming at it from an odd angle, which doesn't make it the easiest job to accomplish. Do you understand?"

Dylan nodded.

"But with you… it's not a performance. I can be myself." He cocked his head. "Does it feel intimate?"

"Yes."

"That's because it is." He pointed to the laptop screen. "*That* is me making love to a beautiful man. No schedule, no planning, nothing but the two of us, enjoying each other."

And if Mark stuck to his guns, there would be

no more videos.

He didn't mind that prospect at all.

Dylan reached over and hit Play, staring at the screen, his lips parted.

Mark leaned over and kissed his neck, and Dylan shivered. Mark nuzzled him there. "Hmm, you smell good."

"I smell clean." Mark's dick jerked, hitting the underside of the laptop, and Dylan chuckled. "But maybe it's time to get dirty again." He grinned. "This time *without* the cameras." He pointed to the coffee table. "Leave it there."

"You sure you don't want me to bring it to the bedroom? For… a visual aid?"

Then Dylan removed the laptop from his lap, set it aside, and knelt on the rug at Mark's feet. "Who said anything about the bedroom?"

October 14

Mark poured himself a cup of coffee and sat at the kitchen table to check his phone. He had to smile when the first text that popped up was from Dylan.

Is it the weekend yet?

Poor baby. He'd been working the night shift, and had just gone to bed. Mark's thumbs flew over the screen. *When you wake up, come over. I'll feed you.* When an eggplant popped up on his screen, Mark laughed out loud. *I'll feed you that too. Now get some sleep.*

His phone rang, and Mark was ready to insist Dylan got some shuteye, until he saw an unknown number. He clicked *Answer.* "Hello?"

"Am I speaking to Michael Thornton?" The male voice sounded older and efficient.

He tensed. "Yes." Christ, he hadn't had anyone call him by his birth name in years.

"My name is Cedric Waterson. I represent the firm of Waterson and Deveraux, and I'm calling about your late grandfather, Derek Willis. I was his lawyer for many years."

"My late—" A sudden feeling of cold spread from his core, and pain lanced through his chest. "When… when did he die?" *I should have called him. I should have known something was wrong.*

"Last week. I'm calling because… Well, your grandfather did share your… situation with me, so I knew there was a likelihood you hadn't been informed of his death or the funeral." He paused. "I'm sorry to be the bearer of such sad tidings."

That was when the full force of the situation hit him. *No one called to tell me. Not one of them.* Loathing surged through him. With a supreme effort, Mark choked back the tears. "When is the funeral?"

"Next Monday. I felt I had to call, to give you sufficient time to arrange transportation. You still reside in Wells, Maine? The address I have for you is 18 Acorn Drive."

"Yes, that's right. And I'll be there." Saying goodbye to Grandpa would come first, then he'd blast those bastards with every bit of venom he possessed.

"There was another reason why I had to ascertain if you'd be present. I need to speak with you, concerning your grandfather's will. You are named as a beneficiary."

"Oh. Oh, I see." That was *so* like Grandpa to think of him. Then Mark realized he knew exactly what Grandpa had left him. *The clock that used to stand in their hallway in Wells. The one Grandpa would let me wind up whenever I stayed with them.*

"Apart from a number of bequests, there are only two major beneficiaries—yourself, and your mother, Rebecca Thornton, née Willis."

That stopped him dead. "Really?"

"If I could have an email address, I'll send you the details for the funeral, which will be in Miami."

Mark rattled it off, and Mr. Waterson repeated it back to him. "How... how did he die?" *Please, God, don't let him have suffered.*

"It was a massive stroke. There was no warning. He was my client for over forty years, and named me his executor. Again, my condolences. I will send details of where we can meet on Monday, or whenever you arrive in Miami. I can always meet you at your hotel."

"Thank you, Mr. Waterson. I'd say I look forward to meeting you, but under the circumstances..."

"Quite. Well, until Monday." Mr. Waterson disconnected.

Mark placed his phone on the table, his head spinning. Regrets about not calling Grandpa were a waste of energy. The last time they'd spoken was the middle of August: Grandpa had called to complain about the heat, and Mark had given his usual reminder that hey, they'd chosen to move to Florida, right?

Tears pricked the corners of his eyes, and

Mark wept for the man who had loved him when no one else had. He fought to regain his self-control, and went in search of his laptop.

He had a flight to book.

It wasn't until he pulled up the airline's page that he realized he didn't want to do this alone. He quickly composed a text.

Call me as soon as you wake up.

When his phone rang less than a minute later, he knew Dylan hadn't put his phone on mute. "What's wrong?" Dylan sounded a little groggy.

"This can wait."

"No, it can't. You think I'm going to sleep after getting that message? What's up?"

"Are you owed any vacation time?"

Dylan snorted. "What's a vacation?"

Thank God. "So if I needed you to ask for some time off at short notice, could you do it?"

"I think I could wrangle it. Why?"

"I have to go to Florida this weekend. My grandpa died. The funeral is Monday and… I don't want to go alone."

"Aw, Mark, I'm so sorry. I know he meant a lot to you. Let me call HR and see what I can do. Where will we stay?"

"I'll book a hotel room, don't worry about that. Thank you." He'd never been more grateful.

"I'll be there for you, okay? I'll call you when I know for sure they're giving me the time off." He disconnected.

Mark closed the laptop. There was no point searching for flights until he knew he was booking for one passenger or two. The temptation to call his parents and tell them what he thought of them was right there—until he remembered his mom had just lost her dad.

    I'll show her more consideration than she's shown me.
    Mark could be the fucking grown-up.

Chapter Nineteen

October 18

Mark thanked the Uber driver, and got out of the car to collect their bags from the trunk. Dylan gazed at the palm trees lining the avenue. As the car drove away, he turned to Mark with a tired smile, gesturing to the hotel. "You know I have to ask this, right?"

Fatigue and apprehension dueled for dominance, and fatigue was winning, but the comment brought a chuckle. "Yes, I *have* used this hotel for a shoot." The Holiday Inn on Miami Beach had been the first place he'd thought of. He'd already informed Mr. Waterson of where they were staying, and the lawyer had replied to say he'd meet Mark in the hotel bar that afternoon.

After we take a nap. It had only been a three-hour flight, but they'd had an early start, and neither of them had gotten much sleep—for once, that had nothing to do with sex, and everything to do with the tumult inside Mark's head. Dylan was doing his best to support him, but Mark was as tense as a piano wire, trying to hold it together until he got through the funeral, and saw his family. Dylan wasn't saying much, and Mark knew that was down to him—his mood didn't invite much conversation—but the touch of Dylan's hand on his back, the warmth in his eyes, even the way he gave Mark some space, said more than words ever could.

Once they'd checked in and gone up to their room, Dylan flopped onto one of the queen beds. "What time does that lawyer get here?"

"Two. So if you want to grab some shuteye, go right ahead. I'll be doing the same."

"Fine, as long as you don't plan on sleeping way over there."

Mark planned on falling asleep with his arms wrapped around Dylan.

"You're sure you don't mind staying up here while I meet Mr. Waterson?" Mark asked, checking his phone.

Dylan sighed. "Of course not. This needs to be just you and him. I'll be waiting for you when you're done."

Mark kissed him. "And tonight you get a choice. We go out to eat, or we order in."

Dylan rolled his eyes. "For an intelligent man, you say some dumb things."

Another kiss, and Mark was out of there, heading for the elevator. There'd been no messages from any of his family, and he had to assume they were in Miami too. *And obviously not expecting to see me.*

Mark had no intention of biting his tongue.

When he reached the bar, he scanned it for someone who had the appearance of an elderly lawyer. He didn't have to look far: a small man in a dark gray suit stood, raising his hand in a wave. Mark hurried over to him, and they shook.

"Mr. Thornton. I recognized you from a photo your grandfather kept. I'm having some tea." Mr. Waterson gestured to the pot on the table. "Would you like some?" Mark accepted the offer, and sat facing him. "Thank you for agreeing to meet," Mr. Waterson said as he poured the fragrant amber liquid into a white cup. "This is a formality that has to be undertaken, and there are official documents that require your signature, as one of the beneficiaries."

"I take it you'll also be meeting with my mom?"

Another nod. "That will be tomorrow, after the funeral. I felt it best to see you separately, given the... present state of affairs."

Which had to be lawyer-speak for 'they don't want anything to do with you.' That was fine by Mark. He wanted nothing to do with them.

Mr. Waterson gave him an inquiring glance. "Did your grandfather ever call you by another name?"

Mark smiled. "No one calls me Michael, except probably my parents and siblings. Grandpa called me Mark, the name I've gone by since I left home. Why do you ask?"

Mr. Waterson took a sip of tea. "You just solved a puzzle for me. I'll explain that in a moment."

"You said on the phone you represented Grandpa for forty years."

He nodded. "I helped him set up his first

company—you know he had many business interests?"

"By the time I'd gotten to know him well, he'd retired."

The lawyer nodded once more. "They moved here for your grandmother's health, and when she passed, he had no wish to leave." He leaned back in his chair. "The house in Wells—you remember that?" Mark gave a nod. "Well, when they left Maine, they didn't sell it, but left it in the hands of a rental agency that has maintained it to this day. The present tenants have been given notice, and once all the relevant paperwork has been finalized, I will send you the details."

Mark frowned. "Why would I need those?"

Mr. Waterson blinked. "Forgive me. I haven't said, have I? Your grandfather has bequeathed to you the house in Wells."

Shock thrummed through him. "I thought… well, I was expecting…"

"What did you think he'd left you?"

Mark forced a smile. "The clock that stood in their hallway."

Mr. Waterson's eyes twinkled. "He did—in a way. That clock was placed in storage when they left Maine, and it is listed in the inventory of items to pass to you, along with the house. He left the house in Miami to your mother, along with monetary bequests to certain named individuals."

"When did he draw up his will?"

"Two years ago." He picked up the briefcase that sat on the floor beside his chair, placed it on the table, opened it, and removed a long white envelope. "I found this when I went through his papers. As I told you, your grandfather died suddenly, so I have no idea when he wrote this." His smile was kind. "And I now know it was for you."

Mark took it, his hand shaking a little. It was addressed simply *to Mark*, and he recognized his grandpa's spidery scrawl immediately. For a moment, he gazed at it.

"He was very fond of you." Mr. Waterson's voice quavered. "He told me to share details of one of his bequests which he said would be of special interest to you." He consulted his notes. "Lost-N-Found Youth, a nonprofit based in Atlanta, I believe, that finds safety and shelter for LGBTQ+ young people."

Mark's throat tightened. "Yes. I was the one who told him about them." He held the envelope against his chest.

Mr. Waterson nodded. "He left them the sum of ten thousand dollars." He peered at Mark. "That's all the information I can give you at the present time. As I said, I will forward all the paperwork once everything is settled, but as the agency contacted the tenants immediately following your grandfather's death, all the details should be in order before the end of this month. I'll have the keys and documents sent to you by courier." He picked up his cup and drank, then reached once more into his briefcase. He placed a manila folder on the table, then removed several sheets of paper. "These require your signature. They simply state that I have passed on the relevant details of the bequest, the letter, and that I will send any documents, keys, et cetera, to you once everything is settled." He separated the sheets, and handed Mark a pen. "Please sign where you see an *X*." He coughed. "I'm afraid I require your birth name. And I'll need to see some ID. Purely a formality."

Mark placed the envelope on the table, and then handed over his ID. He signed his name on three official-looking papers. "I'll be seeing you tomorrow?"

"Of course." Mr. Waterson glanced at the letter. "He only left one such item."

That tightened Mark's throat even more.

He stood, and Mr. Waterson rose too. They shook hands, and Mark left the bar, walking toward the elevators. When the doors slid shut and he found himself alone, he drew a deep breath.

Oh Grandpa. You sweet, sweet man. Mark had so many happy memories tied up in that house.

When he got to their floor, he exited the elevator and headed for the room. Dylan was on the bed, earbuds in, eyes closed, lost to the world. Mark crept over to the balcony and opened the window. He stepped outside and pulled the sliding glass panel shut after him. Mark sat on one of the chairs, gazing out at the ocean. The sun was warm on his face, and the temperature had to be in the eighties.

I can see why they preferred this to Maine. The temperature in Maine was in the low fifties. *Just not sure I could live with it like this.* He was prevaricating and he knew it. Mark slit the envelope with his fingernail, and removed a single piece of folded creamy paper, so familiar to the letters he'd received. Mark opened it, searching for a date. The letter had been written the previous year.

My dear Mark,

I'm not really sure why I decided to write this now, and to be honest, I don't know whether I'll mail it, or leave it for you to read when I'm gone. So either I'm dead, or you're thinking 'I need to call him, because I've never known him to be so maudlin.'

> *I'm going to keep this short.*
> *I'm sorry for all the crap you've had to endure.*
> *I'm sorry for those times when I could have spoken out, and didn't.*
> *I'm sorry we didn't get to spend as much time together these past few years as I would have liked.*
> *I just wanted to make sure you knew what a special man you are. And if my daughter and her idiot husband don't realize that, then they're fools.*
> *And if I can leave you with one thing to hold onto, it's this:*
> *Illegitimi non carborundum.*
> *I know it's not real Latin, but it's the thought that counts— Don't let the bastards grind you down. Don't you change, Mark, not for them.*
> *Love you.*

> *Grandpa*

Mark dropped the letter to the floor and wept, unable to hold in the tears. The fact he'd addressed the letter to Mark and not Michael had unleashed a torrent of sorrow that would not be contained.

He accepted me, when no one else did.

The window slid open. "Hey, you okay?"

Mark gazed up at Dylan's face, noting the concerned expression, and wrapped his arms around his waist, burying his face in the soft cotton of Dylan's shirt, his tears soaking into it.

Dylan kissed the top of his head. "Hey," he said softly, stroking his hair.

Little by little, Mark regained his self-control. He sat back, wiping his eyes, and shuddered out a long breath. "I'm okay now." He reached down and picked up the letter. "This is from Grandpa." He handed it to Dylan, then breathed deeply, letting a new calm wash over him.

Silence fell as Dylan read it, followed by a slow exhale. "Oh. I wish I'd known him. I think I would've liked him."

"He'd have liked you. Every time we spoke, he'd say the same thing… 'Are you dating anyone?' And when I'd say no, he'd make this clicking sound with his teeth, and tell me I shouldn't be so picky about men."

Dylan sat on the chair facing him. "How did the meeting go?"

Mark stared at him. "He left me the house in Wells, the one I thought they'd sold years ago."

"No kidding? Where is it?"

Mark chuckled. "I still have no idea. When the dust has settled, the lawyer will send me all the details."

"He must have loved you a lot."

"He did," Mark admitted. "And I'm going to warn you now… I'm going to be a basket case tomorrow at the funeral. Not because I usually cry at these things, but because it's *his* funeral." His stomach grumbled. "I think I need to eat something."

"Then let's go find someplace to eat, maybe close to the beach?" When Mark gazed at him in surprise, Dylan flushed. "Yeah, I know. You thought I'd wanna eat in here. But it's warm out there and I thought we should make the most of this weather. We couldn't eat outdoors in Maine right now—well, not without patio heaters."

Mark nodded. "I'll change into my shorts."

"There *is* one possible drawback." Dylan bit his lip. "Am I gonna be fighting off guys wanting selfies all the time we're out there?"

Mark sighed. "Possibly?" Then he grinned. "I'll buy myself a hat and I'll wear my shades."

Dylan snorted. "Yeah right. I'd know your body *anywhere*. Just sayin'."

How long will it take after I've left all this behind me, before I can walk down the street and no one gives me a second glance?

Mark was more than ready to be yesterday's news.

October 19

The funeral wasn't going to be as bad as Mark had anticipated.

It was going to be much, much worse.

From the moment he and Dylan got out of the Uber, he could feel eyes boring into him. He spotted his parents instantly, but made no move to go over to them. Dylan had murmured something about being the bigger person, but Mark ignored the comment.

He was *way* past that.

The mourners stood in small groups, talking in low voices. It seemed no one was keen to leave the warm sunshine for the interior of the chapel. Several faces were unknown to him, and he guessed they were people who'd known Grandpa during his time in Florida, or from before he'd retired, judging by the age of some of them.

His parents stood with his brothers and sister, and it took Mark a second or two to realize there were others too: a tall man clutched his sister Beth's hand, and it seemed his brothers had partners too.

Well, so do I.

Mark took Dylan's hand in his, and walked into the small chapel that served the funeral home, ignoring Dylan's short smothered gasp of surprise. The coffin sat at the front, its lid closed, and Mark was grateful for that. He wanted to remember his grandfather the way he'd been the last time Mark had visited. Flowers surrounded the coffin, in wreaths or arranged in displays of white blooms interspersed with small blue flowers, nestled against green leaves.

"Give me a minute, okay?" Mark released Dylan's hand and approached the coffin, coming to a halt in front of it. He bowed his head.

God? You've got a good one there. Look after him. Then he smiled to himself. *And don't play poker with him. He's a card shark.*

"I shouldn't think the Lord listens to the prayers of those who stray from the path He laid out for them."

He froze at his dad's voice, and it took all his effort not to turn to see those eyes so like his own. Except he knew they'd be cold. "Don't talk the talk unless you can walk the walk. I shouldn't think He listens to the prayers of people who only pay Him lip service." He suppressed a shiver. "I don't know about *your* God, but mine is a God of love." He inclined his head toward the coffin. "Now *there* is a man who walked with God."

And *still* Mark couldn't look at him.

He caught his dad's intake of breath, and wasn't about to give him the chance to speak. Mark walked slowly to his seat, shaking.

"Who's that?" Dylan murmured as he sat beside him.

"My dad." Mark didn't offer anything else. Something inside him had begun to tighten like a coiled clock spring, and he didn't trust himself to utter a word.

"Are you okay?"

He glanced at Dylan. "Do you need to ask?"

Dylan blinked, then jerked his head to the front. Around them, the mourners were taking their seats, and Mark noted his family were on the opposite side of the chapel.

Fine by me. He didn't want to be that close to them.

Mr. Waterson was there, his white hair so stark in contrast to his black suit. He gave Mark a nod and a warm smile before sitting toward the rear of the chapel.

It wasn't a long service, but the minister's words came from the heart, and Mark guessed he'd known Grandpa, judging by the humorous remarks that brought chuckles from the assembled crowd. Now and then, Dylan laid his hand gently on Mark's thigh, but Mark's hands were clenched into tight fists. The mourners rose to sing a couple of hymns, and it took Mark a moment to realize Dylan wasn't singing. Then he reasoned not everyone was into hymns. And then it was over, and everyone was filing past the coffin. His family walked out, a tightknit group, no one even giving Mark a second glance.

Mark held his breath until they'd passed by, then let it out in a slow exhale. Beside him, Dylan was silent, so silent that Mark turned to check he was still there. Dylan faced the front of the chapel, his face tight.

"Well, that's that," Mark said with a sigh.

"Do you want to say goodbye to him?"

Mark had already said his goodbyes. "Let's go," he said shortly. Without waiting for a response from Dylan, Mark got up, then walked toward the door, his heart sinking when he caught sight of his family waiting just beyond it.

Waiting for me.

That was fine too. Mark had waited long enough to tell them what he really thought of them.

"Making a point?" Paul's face still bore that same sneer he'd been wearing the day Mark left. He gave the tiniest jerk of his head toward Dylan. "I'm ashamed to call you my brother." The woman next to him gave him a startled glance.

Mark couldn't resist. "But I'm not your brother. You told me that seventeen years ago, remember? *You* may have forgotten what you said, but I certainly haven't."

"You have a lot of nerve, bringing him. I'm glad Grandpa isn't here to see this."

Mark finally understood what people meant by a red mist, because one was descending before his eyes. "Okay, *bro*. Grandpa *is* here, and I for one think he's listening to every word that comes out of your hating big mouth. And I *know* he would have been delighted to meet Dylan. Because he wanted me to be happy." He shuddered. "I don't know why *you* came here, but I came to say goodbye to a man I loved and respected. Except I didn't even know he'd gone, because not *one* of you thought to call me. My phone may have changed many times, but my number sure hasn't, so please, don't make the excuse that you didn't know how to reach me. You didn't even fucking *try*."

"You will *not* talk to anyone in this family using that kind of language," his dad ground out in a harsh whisper. His mom's eyes were red and puffy, and for one moment, Mark's heart went out to her—until he came to his senses, and realized she wasn't contradicting one damn thing his dad and brother were saying.

Mark wasn't about to let them see his tears.

"You know what? I don't want to talk to anyone in this family, period. So I guess we're done—again." Mark strode through the crowd, dimly aware of Dylan trying his best to keep up. He walked along the street, his phone in his hand, multitasking as he searched for an Uber. All he wanted was to put as much distance as possible between himself and his family.

The Uber was on its way, and Mark breathed out all the hostility that had finally bubbled out of whichever dark spot of his soul had held onto it for so long. Then he realized Dylan was staring at him, and he stilled. "Something wrong?"

"Why did you ask me to come with you?"

Chapter Twenty

Mark's puzzled expression only added to Dylan's confusion. "What's wrong?"

Dylan gaped at him. "Seriously? You don't know?" His heart raced, and there was a sinking feeling in his midsection. "You could've told me why you wanted me here. If you'd asked, I'd have said yes."

"I don't understand. Why are you so... pissed?"

Dylan struggled to keep a lid on his emotions. "I'm not pissed, just confused at being invited along to support you, only to have you drag me around and snub me. And if I'm angry with anyone, it's with myself more than you. I got the wrong end of the stick, that's all."

"You're not making any sense."

Another long inhalation. "I didn't know I was here as a Fuck-You to your family. I didn't realize that was why you asked me along."

Mark's shoulders slumped and his mouth fell open, his gaze flat. "Is *that* what you think?"

"What the hell am I supposed to think when you ignore me, snap at me, act like I'm not even here—but make a point of taking my hand when we walked into the chapel?" He gave him a hard stare. "If you were me, what would *you* think?"

Their Uber arrived, and Mark sighed heavily.

"Get in. We'll talk about this when we get back to the hotel, okay?" He laid a hand on Dylan's shoulder. "But I *will* say this—you couldn't be more wrong. And it's my fault you feel this way, so I guess I have some explaining to do."

His words mollified Dylan a little, and his heartbeat climbed back down to somewhere near its usual rhythm. They got into the Uber, but for the duration of the trip to the hotel, Dylan couldn't speak. *I thought he asked me along because he needed me. Because I meant something to him.* He hadn't wanted to believe Mark could be so… unfeeling, but with each passing moment, it was as if a stranger was at Dylan's side.

I'll wait till we're alone.

They arrived at the hotel, and he followed Mark through the crowded lobby to the elevators. When they were finally in their room, Mark shrugged off his suit jacket, tugged his tie loose and removed it, then kicked off his shoes. Before Dylan could open his mouth, Mark got in first.

"I fucked up, didn't I? You were trying to help, I can see that now. The reason I couldn't see it half an hour ago was because that… family of mine put my emotions to the test, and you bore the brunt of my anger and frustration. I had no right to take my misery out on you." He cupped Dylan's cheek. "Did you really think I'd taken you there to rub my family's faces in it?"

Dylan managed a nod.

"So what did you mean about getting the wrong end of the stick?"

Dylan wasn't sure he could go that far, but then he reconsidered. *I've been wanting to know how things are between us for so long—why not come out with it?* There might never be a more opportune moment.

"I hoped you'd asked because you… cared for me. Because I was… important to you."

Mark withdrew his hand and sank onto the edge of the bed. "Yeah, I really have fucked this up."

"No," Dylan remonstrated, sitting beside him. "We're talking, aren't we? It's nothing that can't be fixed, right?"

Please, don't let whatever it is we've got here be broken before we even get the chance to make it work.

Mark laced his fingers with Dylan's and the intimacy of the gesture sent hope hurtling through him. "The thing is," Mark began, "Up until now, I haven't said what I wanted to tell you, out of fear."

That one word lifted the hairs on the back of Dylan's neck.

Mark didn't look at him, but at their joined hands. "There's a reason I'm alone. You already know it. Porn gets in the way."

Dylan began to see the light. "You're saying you've not taken this—*us*—any further because you're scared I can't cope with your *career*? Because I seem to cope just fine."

Mark nodded. "So did all the others—until they reached breaking point." Then he froze, his eyes wide. "But just now I realized something. Yes, I'm scared of asking you to stay—but I'm *more* scared of losing you."

"So where does that leave us?" *Tell me, in words of one syllable, how you feel.* Dylan knew the words he longed to hear, words *he* needed to say too.

Mark's fingers were gentle as he reached over and stroked Dylan's face. "When I walked into that hotel, I had no idea I was about to meet a man who would change my life—but I did know that life had to change. So… if you'll have me… you'd be taking on an *ex*-porn star."

Dylan gaped. "You're quitting?"

Mark nodded again. "Yeah. It's time to call it a day." He locked gazes with Dylan. "And that wasn't the answer I was expecting."

Dylan smiled. "I don't care if you're a porn star, ex-porn star, whatever… I don't want to lose you either." He swallowed. "You changed my life too. *'If I'll have you'*? You really think I could walk away from what we have?"

Mark's breathing hitched, his lips met Dylan's, and Dylan found himself on his back, Mark tugging at his shirt, his belt, his pants.

"Either you think I need to cool off, or you're intent on having your wicked way with me," Dylan quipped. Then he gasped as Mark bared his chest and bent to flick Dylan's nipples with his tongue. "Aw, Christ, yeah."

Mark broke off his sensual onslaught to look Dylan in the eye. "As for my intent, I aim to be inside you in less than five minutes. You got a problem with that?"

Dylan cupped Mark's nape. "None whatsoever." He reached toward the nightstand for the condoms and lube, but Mark stopped him.

"When we land in Portland tomorrow, and I pick up the car from the parking lot, would it be okay if we didn't go straight back to my place?"

Dylan grinned. "What did you have in mind? A tour of the lighthouses?"

"I was thinking more along the lines of a visit to the Frannie Peabody Center." When Dylan frowned, Mark smiled. "It's where I go once a month to get tested. I thought you might like to join me."

Oh fuck.

"I did say we'd talk about this again, didn't I?"

Dylan's pulse quickened. "Yes, but—"

Mark didn't break eye contact. "I said if you'll have me. I meant *all* of me, with nothing between us. No secrets… and no latex." He paused. "How does that sound?"

There was only one answer to that. "Perfect."

"Nothing is perfect." Mark smiled. "Nothing wrong with aiming for it though." His eyes sparkled. "Anything *you'd* like to perfect?"

Dylan bit his lip. "There are a few techniques I'd like to improve on."

"Such as?"

"How fast I can get you out of your clothes."

October 20

Dylan bowed his head under the steady stream of hot water, letting it sluice his fatigue away. He was glad to be back in Maine, but the prospect of work the following day meant more than the return to his usual routine—it brought an end to three days spent totally in Mark's company. The shine hadn't worn off the previous day's declarations. Neither of them had come right out and said the L-word, but Dylan wasn't worried. The funeral had paved the way for a clearer understanding between them.

It wasn't all sunshine and roses though. Then he reasoned that had to be a good thing. Grammy used to say it was a mistake to buy a house in a place you'd only seen in the summer—you needed to see it in all seasons to know if you could really like it there.

I guess I've seen Mark in all his seasons. And hey, guess what? He's not Mr. Perfect.

Yeah, it was definitely a good thing.

He turned off the water and stepped out of the shower. Mark had said something about checking his various sites. Not for the first time, Dylan wondered which direction Mark would take. The decision to quit the porn industry hadn't been all *that* big a shock: the writing had been on the wall for a while, he supposed. But inheriting his grandfather's house had to have taken a load off Mark's mind, in terms of his financial future.

"You done in there? I'm in the kitchen. Won't be a sec."

Dylan wrapped a towel around his hips and walked out of the bathroom. "Yup. I got rid of all my travel cooties."

"Travel—what?"

He cackled. "One of Grammy's sayings. It's her excuse for not going on vacation. I remember Levi coming home from a science class when he was maybe twelve or thirteen, informing her his teacher had told him there was no such thing."

"What did Grammy say?" Mark called out.

Dylan grinned. "Something about how it just went to show someone could get all that education, and still be number than a hake." Then he realized there was something different about Mark's bedroom.

The St. Andrew's Cross set up in the corner might have had something to do with that.

His mouth went dry, and his pulse quickened.

Mark came up behind him. "Did you think I'd forgotten?"

Dylan shook his head. "I just figured you had a lot on your mind, that's all." And what was on his mind right then was the feel of Mark's bare chest against his back.

"Not so much that I could forget you have needs, and I haven't met them yet." Mark leaned in, his breath warm on Dylan's neck. "Now, if you're too tired, I'd understand. We can always do this another ni—"

"Nooo."

Mark turned him slowly so he could no longer see the black cross with its metal loops and sturdy frame, lengths of white rope hanging over its center...

Jesus. We're really gonna do this.

"Look at me."

Dylan shuddered, but met Mark's forthright gaze.

"That's better. Now, if we're going to make this—us—work, then we need to be there for each other." Mark stroked Dylan's nape, sending shivers through him. "You were there for me in Miami, even if I was too messed up to see it right away. And I'm here for you. Because you said something about being helpless... not able to stop me..." His eyes gleamed. "Was that about the size of it?"

Dylan swallowed. "Yes." The word came out as a whisper.

Then Mark pushed him backward, skirting the

bed until his back met the cool surface of the St. Andrew's Cross. "Arms up."

Dylan didn't hesitate, his heart pounding as Mark looped rope around his wrists, then worked the ends through the fastenings at the top of the frame.

"Not too tight?"

Dylan shook his head. *Christ, we really are doing this.* Then Mark gripped his chin, forcing Dylan to look him in the eye.

"Now… anytime you want to stop, say Red, okay?" When Dylan nodded again, Mark's grip tightened. "Uh-uh. Let me hear the words."

"Okay." Dylan gave a hard swallow.

Mark smiled. "You thought all you were getting was a fucking on the pool table?" He leaned in, and his kiss was hot, savage, his palms slapping Dylan's pecs. "Nothing hardcore, like I said." Another brutal kiss, only this time he scraped his nails over Dylan's nipples and chest. "You like that?"

No, Dylan fucking *loved* it.

Mark lowered his gaze and grinned. "Ooh, I seem to have woken something up." Then he locked gazes. "We need to lose this towel." He yanked it from Dylan's body, and Dylan's cock sprang up, hard and wanting. Mark's fingers traced the line of it, and then Dylan sucked in air when he gave it a light smack, followed by another, and another.

"Too much?" Mark demanded.

"Fucking *perfect*."

Mark bent low, cupped Dylan's balls, and gave his dick a hard suck.

"Fuck, yeah."

Mark knelt at his feet, grinning. "I hear that a lot." Dylan's legs shook as Mark sucked on his balls, first one, then the other, then both. He licked the underside of Dylan's shaft, tugging on his sac, and Dylan's tremors increased. Mark's head bobbed as he pulled hard on Dylan's balls, stretching the skin, and when he reached for the lube to slick up a finger, Dylan's heart hammered.

"Do it," he urged.

Mark's eyes twinkled. "Do I need to stuff my jock in your mouth? My dirty, sweaty jock that I wore all the way home from Miami?"

Dylan gaped. "How the fuck do you know just what to say to get my motor revving?"

He grinned. "I told you. I pay attention." Then that finger was in his ass, and Mark was clearly taking no prisoners. He swallowed Dylan's shaft to the root, his finger moving in and out of him, in harmony with his mouth, until Dylan was shaking, trembling, his body *zinging* as he shot his load, unable to rein it back. He grabbed the ropes and hung there, too zapped to stand upright.

Mark unfastened his bonds, rubbing his wrists. He led Dylan to the bed, and Dylan flopped onto his back, his chest rising and falling. Blood pounded in his ears, and his stomach quivered.

"Wow," he said weakly.

"Good wow?" Mark lay beside him.

"Oh yeah."

Mark kissed his chest. "Good. Because we're only just getting started." He paused. "But before we do, there's something I need to say."

Dylan's heartbeat quickened, and he had no idea why. "Oh? That sounds serious."

"It is. And that's why I need to say it *now*, not when I'm balls-deep inside you, but when I'm looking you in the eye, so you know I mean every word of it."

Jesus, his heart…

Mark took a deep breath. "I love you, Dylan Martin. I love your sense of humor, your quirks, your kinks—all of them. You're not the first guy I've said these words to, but hand on heart, I mean every goddamn word, and I want you to be the *last* guy I ever say them to. And I don't care if you think it's too soon to be—"

Dylan stopped his words with a kiss. "You had me at 'I love you.'"

Chapter Twenty-One

October 28

Mark signed for the official-looking envelope, then closed the door. He walked into the bedroom, smiling as he caught Dylan singing in the shower.

Someone sounds happy this morning.

Mark knew the feeling, not that it made much logical sense. He had no income, no job prospects on the horizon, and yet he woke every morning feeling lighter than he'd felt for a long time. His days began the same way—holding Dylan, kissing Dylan, making love to Dylan…

It doesn't get much better than this.

He sat on the bed, tapping the envelope against his fingers. He knew what it contained, of course—options. Because if Grandpa's house was finally his, that was an asset he hadn't counted on, something to take the pressure off while he searched for a job to pay his bills. Whether Grandpa had intended him to live in it, or sell it, Mark had no idea, but the end result was the same—financial security.

"Is that what I think it is?" Dylan asked as he emerged from the steam-filled bathroom.

Mark laughed. "How is it I can take a shower in three minutes' flat, leaving no condensation, while *you're* in there for anything from ten minutes to twenty, and the walls end up dripping."

"I can always shower at home," Dylan suggested. "I was going to, remember, until *someone* said, 'No, no, have a shower here.' Now, why was that?" His eyes sparkled as he dropped the towel from around his hips. "Might it have something to do with this?"

His dick made Mark's mouth water.

Then Mark cleared his throat. "Yes, it might. And yes, this is what you think it is." He tore the envelope open and removed the folded document. "I finally have an address." He sighed. "I could've had it sooner if I'd wanted to call my mom or my dad, but I was in no hurry."

Dylan sat beside him, and Mark was momentarily distracted by the sight of Dylan's cock. "So? Reveal all. Where is this palace you've inherited?"

Mark laughed. "It's hardly that. Says here it's a three-bedroomed house with a back yard." The photo brought the memories flooding back. The dark blue cedar shakes were the same shade he remembered, and above the rooftop he caught sight of the tall trees that marked the plot's boundaries.

"Which is better than nothing. Now, tell me where it is before I have to smack you."

Mark arched his eyebrows. "Excuse me? I'm the only one around here who smacks, remember? *You* are the smackee." Then he peered at the address and smiled. "Of course. Post Road. *That* was it."

Dylan gasped. "Let me see that." He peered at the document. "Oh my God. I don't believe this."

"What is it?"

Dylan pointed to the property next door, the edge of which could just be seen in the photo. "See that house there? With the pale blue cedar?"

"Yes."

Dylan grinned. "That's where Levi lives with Grammy."

It was Mark's turn to gape. "No way." Dylan merely nodded, still grinning. Mark stared at him. "How long have they lived there?"

"Grammy raised Levi from a baby, and she's lived there forever. Everyone in Wells knows her."

"But…" Mark did the math. "That means… the little boy I talked to over the fence…"

"Was Levi." Dylan's jaw dropped. "Okay, this is just too weird. Now I can't wait for Saturday."

Mark blinked. "Why? What's happening on Saturday?"

Dylan bit his lip. "Oh shit. I totally forgot."

"Something you'd like to share?"

Dylan flushed. "Every Halloween, Levi has a party… and we're invited."

"*We* are? He knows about me?"

"I kinda… came out to him as bi a few weeks ago, and yes, he knows. Except he doesn't know much, apart from your name and age. He told me to bring you along. He also said no one has to know we're more than friends."

Warmth trickled through him. "But we're so much more than that, aren't we?"

Dylan's smile reached his eyes. "Duh."

"Just checking."

Dylan laughed. "It's only been a week since you told me you loved me. Did you think I'd forgotten?"

"No, but maybe *I'm* feeling insecure. Maybe I need reassurance." Then he caught his breath as Dylan gently removed the documents from his hand, placed them on the bed, and straddled Mark's lap, looping his arms around Mark's neck.

"I love you." Dylan's lips were warm against his. Mark's hands were at his back, stroking, caressing, shifting lower to cup his ass. Dylan's gaze met his. "And you don't have to go."

"You don't want me to?"

"Well..." Dylan coughed. "It's just that... there will be a couple of my friends who will... recognize you."

It took Mark a moment to fully comprehend his meaning. "Oh." He shook his head. "You want to hear something strange? My first thought when you said that was, 'Why would they? I'm not a porn star anymore.'"

Dylan laughed. "Seb's boyfriend Marcus knew your name in a heartbeat, so it stands to reason Seb will know too. I don't know about Finn, Joel, Ben, Wade, or even Levi." Then his smile faded. "I mean it. I don't want you feeling awkward."

Mark kissed him. "I'm more concerned about you."

"Me?"

"This party could prove eventful." He gave Dylan a speculative glance. "But I suppose that will depend on how much you want to share with them."

"I've thought about that." Dylan sighed. "I've been in hiding for way too long. I don't want to hide anymore."

Mark took Dylan in his arms. "Have I told you lately how proud I am to have you in my life?"

Dylan's lips were soft against his. "Tell me again. Better yet... show me." When Mark's phone vibrated into life, he groaned. "Someone has really crap timing."

Mark laughed. "Oh, come on. I could get calls at any time when you're here and it would be crap timing." He glanced at the screen, and smiled. "But I have to take this one."

"Do I need to put clothes on?"

He rolled his eyes. "To quote you... For an intelligent man, you say some dumb things." He got up from the bed and went into the living room, clicking *Answer* as he walked. "Well, hello, soon-to-be newlywed."

Casey laughed. "Forty-eight hours, give or take, and counting. And I'm calling to thank you for the gift. Not that I've opened it yet, but I'm not worried. You always did have excellent taste."

"I gather I'm still not invited?" He didn't mind so much now. *What do you know? Time* does *heal wounds.* Maybe not all of them, but enough.

"Aw, Mark... I wish you *could* be here, but..."

Mark sat on the couch. "Not even if I turned up with my boyfriend?"

The silence that followed made Mark wish he could see Casey's expression. Then he caught a sharp intake of breath. "Seriously?"

"Well, you did say get a life, so I got one."

"Ohhh. That's awesome news. Tell me about him. How did you meet? *When* did you meet, more importantly? Is it since I last saw you?"

"A lot's happened since your visit. For one thing, I made a discovery."

"What?"

He smiled to himself. "The career of a porn star does have an expiration date after all."

Another shocked silence ensued. "Oh my

God. You quit."

"Yup. Just keep stalking—I mean, following—me, and you'll see. I'm going to tell all my fans."

"No going back?"

"No. Whatever happens, I'm done."

Casey sighed. "I am *so* freaking happy for you."

"And should I still be happy for *you*?"

There was a pause. "I love him. And I'm *going* to love him for as long as I have breath in this body."

"I know exactly how you feel." Mark glanced up at Dylan who stood in the doorway in Mark's robe. Mark beckoned to him, and Dylan joined him on the couch. "Okay, I have to go. I have something cooking. Be happy, sweetheart."

"I will. And you too. Call me again soon? You haven't told me a thing about him."

"I was thinking of inviting you to stay, so you can meet him. Not right now, of course. You'll be on your honeymoon." *And by the time you get back, I could have a new address.*

"I can't wait. I'll send you some wedding pics."

Mark said his goodbyes, and disconnected. He held out his arm, and Dylan moved in for a cuddle. "Now, where were we?"

Dylan craned his neck for a kiss, and it was the perfect response.

October 31

"I still can't believe it," Dylan murmured, staring at the house. The Uber had departed, and they were gazing at Mark's inheritance.

The party wasn't going anywhere.

"You and me both." Mark's hand was at his back. "I was thinking about coming back tomorrow for a proper look. Want to come with me?"

"I'd love to."

Mark glanced toward the house next door. "Do you think Levi or Grammy will remember me?"

Dylan huffed. "I have more pressing issues to think about. I'm about to walk into a party with my boyfriend." He shook his head. "At least I'm on trend." When Mark gave him an inquiring glance, he continued. "Three of my friends surprised the hell out of us when they turned up with partners. Except no one would have been shocked to see them with a guy. Me, on the other hand…"

"You said you were ready for this, but you *are* allowed to change your mind. Whatever you decide, I've got your back."

"I know," Dylan said in a low voice. He let out an exaggerated sigh. "Come on. Let's do this." They walked along the white fence to Grammy's house, and Dylan led Mark up the path to the front door.

Dylan rang the doorbell, and Levi opened it, dressed in a skeleton costume complete with mask. "Hey, Levi."

"How did you know it was me?" He removed the mask.

Dylan chuckled. "Most skeletons don't have beards."

Levi rolled his eyes. "Well, I'm not gonna

shave it off, just for one night." He gave Mark a warm smile. "And you must be Mark. Hi." His brow furrowed. "Have we met?"

"Can we discuss this indoors please?" Dylan demanded. "I'm freezing my nuts off out here."

They stepped into the warm interior, and Levi closed the door. He glanced at their casual clothing. "Okay, I give up. What did you come as?"

Dylan nudged Mark. "This was his idea. Not original—he got it from a movie."

Mark grinned. "We're psychopaths. They look just like everyone else."

Levi chuckled. "Well, you'll fit right in, because no one else came in costume either." Another eye-roll. "Psychopaths. Nice try." Then he was back to staring at Mark. "I'm sure I know your face from somewhere. It wasn't high school, I know that much."

"I'll give you a clue. We used to play ball over your back yard fence, until the day I threw it with too much vigor, and it went through a pane of glass in your grandmother's greenhouse. After that, all we could do was talk."

Levi's eyes widened. "Oh my God. I *remember* you. Except…I'm pretty sure your name wasn't Mark."

"But it is now," Dylan said in a firm voice.

Levi gaped. "You were, what, fifteen? Sixteen? I thought you were so cool." Then he cocked his head. "No, that's not it. I know you from someplace else, I'm certain of it." He smiled. "It'll come to me." He beckoned. "Step this way. Grammy's opened the doors between the living room and the dining room, and everyone's crammed in there. Too damn cold to be outside."

Dylan and Mark followed him toward the double doors, from behind which came laughter and chatter. Dylan paused at the threshold. "Ready?"

"As I'll ever be." Mark kissed his cheek, and Levi let out a soft *aw*. Then the doors opened, and it was showtime.

Seb and Marcus were the first ones Dylan saw. Seb took one look at Mark, and his jaw dropped.

"Oh my fu—"

With a swiftness that left Dylan in awe, Marcus covered Seb's mouth with his hand. "I have one word for you—Grammy." Then he withdrew it slowly before stepping forward to greet them. "It's Mark, isn't it? I'm Marcus, and the guy with the big mouth is my boyfriend, Seb."

Seb was still staring at Mark, open-mouthed.

Dylan couldn't resist. "Will you stop drooling over my boyfriend, please?"

Crickets.

Seb grinned. "You sneaky little fucker," he whispered.

Mark burst out laughing. "Wow. I guess we're not hiding a damn thing."

Dylan had apparently opened the floodgates.

"Your *what?*"

"Since when?"

"You dark horse."

"It's *always* the quiet ones."

Levi stared at Mark, his brow furrowed once more. Then his eyes widened. "Oh God. *Now* I know where I've seen you before." His gaze darted to where Grammy sat in her rocker. "But can we not mention that, please?" He lowered his voice. "I know she's pretty liberal-minded, but this might be *too* liberal, if you catch my drift."

"But I wanna know everything," Seb wailed.

Dylan gave a loud cough. "Guys? We just got here, okay? And we've got all night to answer questions, but right now I need a drink."

"Nice try," Seb said with a cackle. "If you think *that's* gonna hold us at bay, you're delusional." He strolled over to Mark. "Well, hell-*o* there."

"Seb. Behave." Marcus's voice was a mixture of warning and amusement.

"Have we met somewhere?" That was Ben and Finn, almost at the same time.

Dylan turned toward Mark. "I get the feeling it's going to be a long night."

"I see you really did take my advice," Marcus murmured to Dylan as he helped himself to a glass of punch. "By the way, what is in this stuff? It tastes strong."

Dylan cackled. "It doesn't start out that way. It's sort of a tradition around here. Grammy makes this nice, innocent fruit punch, and then we all come along. Everyone adds something, and it ends up being this brew that could take your head off."

"And Grammy doesn't notice?"

He laughed even louder. "Are you kidding? She even waits a few hours before trying it, so she knows we've all done our thing. Mind you, she only has half a glass. And here's my advice. A little goes a long way." He glanced over to where Mark was in deep conversation with Levi. "Do you think everyone knows by now?"

Marcus snorted. "What, with Seb around? Hell yes."

"But no one has said anything."

Marcus cleared his throat. "That might have something to do with the fact that Grammy hasn't gone to bed yet. Give 'em time." He raised his glass. "*You* are the hero of the hour."

"What did I do?"

"Where do I begin? You came out as bi. You found a beautiful man. *And* you snagged yourself a porn star." Marcus grinned. "And I thought you were quiet." He buffed his nails against his shirt. "Of course, I take some credit in all this."

Dylan chuckled. "Yeah, well, you did say 'Explore, Dream, Discover'." He took another look at Mark who was heading for the kitchen with Levi. "I explored my sexuality, I dreamed of finding happiness, and I discovered it in the hotel where I work." Then he gazed inquiringly at Marcus. "What about you? How did things work out with your nephew?"

Marcus's smile died. "I know what's been going on now, at least, but…" His face tightened. "He hasn't chosen an easy path. His heart is telling him one thing, and his head, another. Not sure what's going to happen there. All I know is, I'll be there for him if he needs me."

Dylan gave Marcus a hug. "And *that* tells me you belong here. Because that's what we do."

What came to mind was Shaun and his dad.

Shaun's path isn't easy either.

"You okay?" Marcus squeezed his shoulder.

Dylan nodded. "Just thinking about one of us who could use some support."

"Like your boyfriend."

He frowned. "Huh?"

Marcus grinned. "Seb is moving toward the kitchen. He's choosing a circuitous route to get there, I'll give him that, but he's not fooling me for an instant. You'd better head him off at the pass."

"What—again? He's like a moth to a flame." He chuckled. "I'll go save Mark."

Except he had a feeling Mark could take care of himself.

"I still can't get over this." Levi shook his head. "By the way, do you know how old I was when Grammy finally returned that ball to me? The one she confiscated from us? Sixteen."

Mark laughed. "I'm sorry?"

"And are we going to be neighbors?"

Mark hadn't come to any firm decisions on that, although he was moving in a certain direction. "If we are, I'll count myself lucky."

Levi passed Mark a slice of cake, made in the shape of a jack-o'-lantern. "So… Dylan says you're giving up your… career."

Mark nodded. "Though what I'm going to do to replace the income, I haven't quite worked out yet." He ate a forkful, and his taste buds exploded. "This is amazing."

"Grammy makes one every year."

"At least you don't have to worry about working it all off tomorrow," Dylan said as he approached them. He broke off a piece of Mark's cake with his fingers and shoved it in his mouth.

"Oh, I'm pretty sure I know how I'll be doing that," Mark confided. Then he patted Dylan on the back. "It's a bitch when cake crumbs go down the wrong way, isn't it?" He was having a great time. He had a feeling at least three of Dylan's friends had rumbled who he was, but they hadn't said a word. Seb was obviously dying to say something, but his boyfriend Marcus kept him on a tight leash.

That was another thing he really liked—the differing ages. Meeting a couple of guys in their forties had been a pleasant surprise.

"I've seen your website," Levi announced in a low tone. "Very nice."

"Thanks, I think."

Dylan leaned in. "That's what Levi does. He's a social media manager for a lot of different people and companies. Plus, he maintains websites, keeping them up to date."

"A skill you obviously share," Levi added. He caught his breath. "Hey, wait a minute…"

Mark's skin prickled when both Levi and Dylan stared at him, their eyes bright. "What?"

Dylan was almost buzzing. "How many indie performers do you know?"

Mark snorted. "So many that I couldn't

possibly count them all?"

"And they all do what you do—did—right? Promote themselves, post on social media, upload videos, take bookings…"

"Yeah." Then Mark saw the light. "Oh."

Levi nodded with enthusiasm. "You see where Dylan's going with this, don't you? What you've been doing successfully for yourself all these years, you could do for others."

"You always said it was a pain in the ass to have to spend so much time on that side of the business. So…" Dylan gave a triumphant smile. "Why don't you offer your services to others who feel the same way?"

Levi was still nodding. "You'd still be self-employed, you know the industry… Sounds like the perfect solution."

Mark really liked the idea. "I think you've both got something."

"Got what?" Seb poked his head around the kitchen door.

"We're giving Mark ideas for alternative careers," Levi explained.

Seb widened his eyes. "Really? Why would he want to do that?"

Mark laughed. "I hate to disappoint you, but this has been a long time coming."

"Don't do anything hasty, okay? Just saying…" Then Seb disappeared from view.

"I'll go see if anyone else wants more cake." Levi left the kitchen.

Mark took advantage of the situation. He pulled Dylan toward him. "You are one smart man, do you know that?"

Dylan flushed. "I'm just happy you like the idea."

"And you still want to come back here tomorrow to look at the house?"

He nodded. "At least you'll already know your neighbors. That's if you decide to live in it and not sell it."

Mark had been thinking about that too. "If I were going to sell, it would be the one on Acorn Drive." He couldn't part with the house next door.

I was happy there once. And he intended to be happy there again.

Epilogue

"Well, what do you think?" Mark gestured to the smallest bedroom at the rear of the house. French doors opened to allow access to the back yard.

Dylan rubbed his chin. "I think all of it needs some renovation."

Mark had to agree. The property had been well-maintained, but it was sadly outdated.

"But I have an idea about that." Dylan smiled. "Talk to Finn. He'd be perfect for a job like this."

"Hmm." Mark stroked his beard. "Doesn't asking one of your friends to do this sound a little like nepotism?"

"How do you work that out?"

Mark grinned. "Finn's family, isn't he?" Dylan's laughter lifted him. "Well, it's true. Little did I realize when I took you on, that—"

"Took *me* on?" Dylan's hands were on his hips, his eyebrows heading toward his hairline. "I think you have that backwards."

Mark wouldn't argue with that. "As I was saying, little did I realize you came with seven brothers."

Dylan wagged his finger. "Uh-uh. My family is growing all the time. Who knows who will be added next?" His eyes gleamed. "A sister would be nice. And now, do you want to hear my other idea, or don't you?"

"There's more?" Mark had an idea of his own, one that had been buzzing around his head for the past week.

Dylan looked at their surroundings. "Remember when you gave me the first of many massages?" Mark nodded. "And I said you could add another string to your bow, if you wanted."

"Yes, I remember."

"As soon as I saw this room, I knew what it would be perfect for." Dylan smiled. "A therapy room. Soft music, candles, a massage table... Once you've gotten some training, of course, but you'd be a natural." He pointed to the French doors. "In summer, you could open those, and there'd be the wonderful scent of honeysuckle and jasmine coming from the yard."

Mark couldn't hold back his own smile. "Honeysuckle? Jasmine? I don't recall seeing them out there."

"They're not—yet—but we can change that next spring."

"'We'?" Mark couldn't have wished for a better lead-in. "Funny you should say that. There's something I've been meaning to discuss with you." He walked over to Dylan and pulled him into his arms. "I agree the place needs renovating, but I'd like your input."

"Mine?"

Mark kissed the tip of Dylan's nose. "Yours. Because your opinion matters."

Dylan's face glowed. "Oh."

"And I thought you'd want to help shape this place, seeing as you'll be here a lot—I hope."

Dylan became so still. "Are you asking what I *think* you're asking?"

Mark's heartbeat quickened. "The way I see it, you can either stay where you are, with three slobs who drive you crazy, *or*... you could move in with me. I'm house-trained, I don't leave messes everywhere, and I cook." Another gentle kiss. "I'm not saying move in tomorrow—because even *I'm* not moving in tomorrow—but maybe once this place looks like a home... I'd like you to make it *your* home." His pulse was rapid as he studied Dylan's face for some sign.

Dylan's smile was wonderful to see. "Any place where you are? Feels like home." Then he cocked his head. "About that pool table... Would it be coming with you when you move?"

Mark laughed. "Hell yeah. You think I'd leave that behind? Besides, I think it needs more interesting... stains." Dylan's flushed cheeks were adorable.

"And all your gym equipment?"

"I'll keep some of it. The rest, I'll sell." He smiled. "And you know what else will be coming with me? Something you'll find very useful?"

Dylan bit his lip. "Your toy box?"

He snorted. "I was thinking more about my left-handed can opener, left-handed scissors, vegetable peeler..." Dylan guffawed. "You may laugh, but these things are important." He leaned in and kissed Dylan's neck. "The toy box, the sling, the St. Andrew's Cross... they're going in our bedroom."

Dylan's shiver was delicious.

Then Dylan's phone buzzed, and he sighed. "One sec." He pulled his phone from his pocket, and laughed. "I think we lost track of time. Seb's just seen your video."

"What does he say?" Mark had scheduled the video's release so he didn't have to think about it.

Dylan laughed. "'He quit? Dude, seriously? How am I ever gonna bring my fantasy to life if Mark Roman quits porn?'" He snorted. "I can see Marcus having something to say about that."

"Want to go back to my place and watch it?"

Dylan chuckled. "I saw it when you recorded it, remember? I was standing behind the camera. But I did have an idea about what we could do…"

"Another idea? You're full of those today."

"I thought about revisiting some of my favorite Mark Roman videos… except *recreating* might be a better word."

Mark arched his eyebrows. "Got any videos in mind?"

The flush that rose up Dylan's neck was cute. "Well… there *was* this one with a sling…"

Mark's evening was looking better by the minute. "I think that could be arranged."

Dylan's eyes sparkled. "And then we could talk about this place. Maybe make some plans."

Much as he relished the idea of getting Dylan in his sling, the prospect of discussing changes to the house filled him with much stronger emotions.

Hope.

Gratitude.

Love.

The End

Coming next in the Maine Men series!

Shaun's Salvation (Maine Men Book 5)

Romance is the last thing Shaun wants – but what if it's exactly what he needs – and deserves?

A selfless son barely holding on

Shaun doesn't have much of a life. When he's not working in the restaurant in Portland, Maine, he's home looking after his dad, who has dementia. The only people he sees on a regular basis are his coworkers, and Nathan, his dad's in-home nurse, except he and Shaun are like ships that pass in the night. And on those dark nights when Shaun feels so alone, thoughts of Nathan are all he has to cling to.

A caring nurse

It didn't take Nathan five minutes to know Shaun is a special guy. He's dealt with enough indifferent families to recognize Shaun has and will always put his dad first. That's why Nathan is willing to go above and beyond – Shaun is worth it. Nathan's attraction to him has to go on the back burner, not that Shaun has noticed: Shaun's focus is all on his dad.

Maybe it's time for Nathan to convince Shaun he can keep that focus and still have a life – a life that includes love.

THANK YOU

As always, a huge thank you to my beta team. Where would I be without you?

And a special thank you to Jason Mitchell. You ROCK. You have so much going on in your own life, and you still find time to talk with me, bounce ideas back and forth… usually before dawn.

ALSO BY K.C. WELLS

Learning to Love
Michael & Sean
Evan & Daniel
Josh & Chris
Final Exam

Sensual Bonds
A Bond of Three
A Bond of Truth

Merrychurch Mysteries
Truth Will Out
Roots of Evil
A Novel Murder

Love, Unexpected
Debt
Burden

Dreamspun Desires
The Senator's Secret
Out of the Shadows
My Fair Brady
Under The Covers

Lions & Tigers & Bears
A Growl, a Roar, and a Purr

Love Lessons Learned
First
Waiting for You
Step by Step
Bromantically Yours
BFF

Collars & Cuffs
An Unlocked Heart
Trusting Thomas
Someone to Keep Me (K.C. Wells & Parker Williams)
A Dance with Domination
Damian's Discipline (K.C. Wells & Parker Williams)
Make Me Soar
Dom of Ages (K.C. Wells & Parker Williams)
Endings and Beginnings (K.C. Wells & Parker Williams)

Secrets – with Parker Williams
Before You Break
An Unlocked Mind
Threepeat
On the Same Page

Personal
Making it Personal
Personal Changes

More than Personal
Personal Secrets
Strictly Personal
Personal Challenges

Personal – The Complete Series

Confetti, Cake & Confessions

Connections
Saving Jason
A Christmas Promise
The Law of Miracles
My Christmas Spirit
A Guy for Christmas

Island Tales
Waiting for a Prince
September's Tide
Submitting to the Darkness

Lightning Tales
Teach Me
Trust Me
See Me
Love Me

A Material World
Lace

Satin
Silk
Denim

Southern Boys
Truth & Betrayal
Pride & Protection
Desire & Denial

Maine Men
Finn's Fantasy
Ben's Boss
Seb's Summer

Kel's Keeper
Here For You
Sexting The Boss
Gay on a Train
Sunshine & Shadows
Watch and Learn
My Best Friend's Brother
Bears in the Woods
Princely Submission
Double or Nothing
Back from the Edge
Lose to Win
Teasing Tim
Switching it up
Out for You
State of Mind

Anthologies

<u>Fifty Gays of Shade</u>
Winning Will's Heart

<u>Come, Play</u>
Watch and Learn

<u>Writing as Tantalus</u>
Damon & Pete: Playing with Fire

ABOUT THE AUTHOR

K.C. Wells lives on an island off the south coast of the UK, surrounded by natural beauty. She writes about men who love men, and can't even contemplate a life that doesn't include writing.

The rainbow rose tattoo on her back with the words 'Love is Love' and 'Love Wins' is her way of hoisting a flag. She plans to be writing about men in love - be it sweet or slow, hot or kinky - for a long while to come.

Printed in Poland
by Amazon Fulfillment
Poland Sp. z o.o., Wrocław